WHERE HAVE THEY GONE?

WHERE HAVE THEY GONE?

A Faye Chambers Cosy Crime Mystery II

SUSAN WILLIS

Copyright c 2025 by Susan Willis All Rights reserved. No part of this novel may be reproduced in any form by any means, electronic or mechanical (including but not limited to the Internet, photocopying, recording), or stored in a database or retrieval system, without prior written permission from the author. This includes sharing any part of the work online.

Susan Willis assets her moral right as the author of this work in accordance with the Copyright, Designs and Patent Act 1988.

The characters, premises, and events in this book are fictitious. Names, characters, and plots are a product of the author's imagination. Any similarity to real persons, living or dead, is coincidental and not intended by the author.

Also By Susan Willis:
Deirdre's Tangle
Payback at the Guest House
Cosy Christmas Stocking Fillers
Confession is Good or the Soul
Intriguing Journeys at Christmas
Joseph is Missing
Death at the Caravan Park
The Curious Casefiles
Magazine Stories from the North East
Christmas Shambles in York
Clive's Christmas Crusades
The Christmas Tasters
The Guest for Christmas Lunch
The Man Who Loved Women
Dark Room Secrets
His Wife's Secret
The Bartlett Family Secrets
Northern Bake Off
You've Got Cake
A Business Affair
Is He Having an Affair
NO, CHEF, I Won't!

Map of Birtley - Courtesy of DB Lasercraft
@db.lasercraft.2024

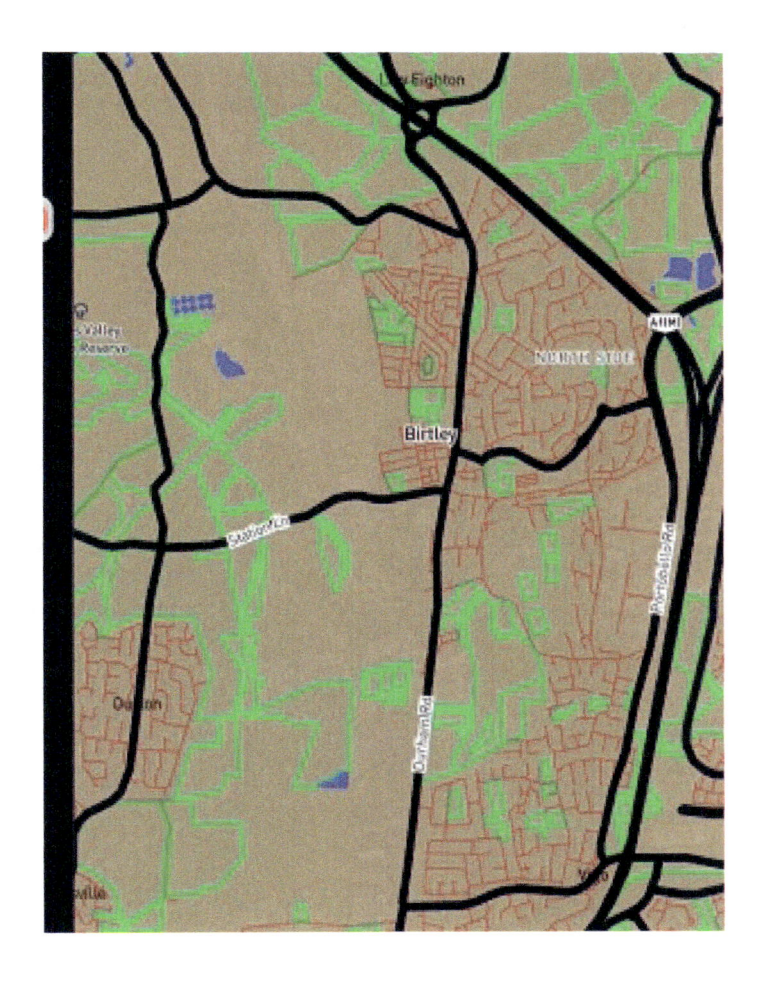

This book is dedicated to my mam, Mrs Mary Willis who has lived in Birtley all her life.

She is the kindest of women and has supported me all the way in my writing journey.

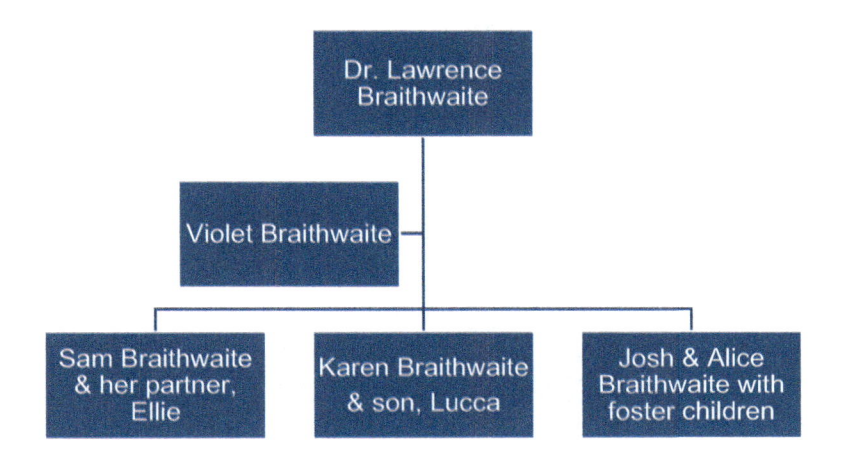

```
                    Dr. Lawrence
                     Braithwaite
                          |
 Violet Braithwaite ──────┤
                          |
  ┌───────────────────────┼───────────────────────┐
Sam Braithwaite      Karen Braithwaite      Josh & Alice
& her partner,         & son, Lucca         Braithwaite with
    Ellie                                   foster children
```

CHAPTER ONE
Faye Chambers is on the case 26.6.2025

I'm stepping out of the shower, envisaging a quiet day at home in South Shields, when my mobile rings. I tut at the interruption.

I answer and hear a woman's voice asking if I'm Faye Chambers.

'Yes, that's me,' I say.

My niece, Zoe, rang yesterday to say that her friend's family were in total chaos because their elderly parents were missing, and she'd given Karen my number.

'But where have they gone?' the woman wails down the phone. 'I mean, two elderly people couldn't just vanish into thin air!'

I frown, knowing this must be Karen, and listen to the woman choking back tears on the other end of the line.

'Look, Karen, take a deep breath and tell me exactly what happened,' I soothe. 'Then maybe I can try to do something to help.'

I hear her inhale deeply and imagine her dropping her shoulders. Zoe had said that Karen was a kind but very organised and restrained woman, so I'm not expecting hysterics. However, I can hear the concern in her trembling voice when she continues.

'W… well, last Tuesday, I sent Mam a text message th… then when there was no answer, I rang to no avail and left her a voice message.'

'Okay, and this was out of character for her?'

'Totally,' she said. 'Mam always rings or replies, no matter where she is or what she's doing.'

'Right, and this was when you suspected something was wrong?'

I can hear by her voice that recounting the beginning of her tale is helping to calm her thoughts.

'So, I rang my brother, Josh, and my younger sister, to see if they'd heard from them, but they hadn't. Sam said the same thing – that she'd messaged Mam a photograph but got no response.'

I probe, 'And then what?'

'Well, Josh and I went up to their house the next morning, and the car had gone - there was no sign of them! We rang around everyone we could think of who knows Mam and Dad, but no one had seen them lately. That's when we rang the police to report them missing.'

With my mobile tucked into my shoulder near my ear, I start to jot down a few notes.

'And you all live near each other?'

I can almost see the smile now on Karen's face as she says, 'Yeah, sorry, I should've told you that first. We're the Braithwaite family here in Birtley and run the oldest funeral business in the town. We all live here apart from young Sam, who lives over in Newcastle.'

I'm scribbling and nodding to myself as I get a sense of the situation. My fingers begin to twitch - this sounds really interesting, the type of mystery which I'd love to get involved with. 'Well, Karen, I've no experience in tracing missing people, but am willing to help if I can.'

I hear the relief in her voice. 'Okay, so Zoe told Sam you'd been successful in South Sheilds finding a murderer. Anything you can do to help us at this stage would be great because the police investigation seems to have come to grinding halt!'

Silently, I curse Zoe for building me up like this to Karen, although I shouldn't complain.

I know how proud my family are of what I've done. I decide it's best to lower Karen's expectations. 'Er, I helped the police inspector piece clues together and, eventually, we found the criminal. But I have to say, it was more good luck than investigative prowess.'

There's a brief silence between us, then Karen says, 'Well, I don't think the police are taking this seriously, so, could you come through to see us in Birtley?'

I nod to myself, knowing it's best to be there and experience the dilemma firsthand rather than relying on emails and phone calls. And, to find out exactly what the police are doing about their disappearance.

'Yes, Karen, I can. Whenever you're ready, I'll drive over to see you and try to get a handle on the situation.'

Karen cries, 'Oh, that's great! Don't suppose you could come over this afternoon?'

I agree, and we arrange a time to meet at her house. I jot down her post code for my sat nav and decide to stop overnight somewhere in Birtley.

'And, of course,' Karen says, 'we'll pay for any expenses and your fee.'

I end the call after saying, 'Lets talk about that this afternoon.'

***

After packing a small bag with overnight necessities, I jump into my little red Mini, fastening my beloved, spaniel, Alfie, into his harness on the back seat. I talk to him all the while, stroking his silky, long ears, which he loves. Entering Karen's post code into the sat nav, I turn the ignition and wonder if I should have asked if it was okay to bring Alfie. However, I smile. Where I go, he goes. I shrug - most people like dogs, don't they?

It's a lovely sunny afternoon in June, and I put on my sunglasses while talking to the sat nav, which, after the first time I used it, I decided she sounded like someone called Doris.

Driving long distances is not something I'm used to or particularly enjoy, but from my new flat in South Shields, the journey should take me around thirty to forty minutes - if Doris keeps me on the right track, of course.

Over, the last year, since I turned fifty-six, there have been a few new developments in my life. Alongside the flat, I now have a new partner called John. Although I love my place overlooking North Marine Park, I spend much of my time at John's house near Souter Lighthouse. He is the friendly police inspector I fell for a year ago whilst solving the case in a guest house on Ocean Road, the one Karen had mentioned earlier.

As I drive along the Coast Road, the traffic builds up, and I wait patiently in the queue. Looking to the right, I recognise the turn-off to Gosforth, a route I used to drive all the time when I lived there. I spent nearly thirty years of my life in Gosforth with my husband and family - until last year, when my marriage to Allan irretrievably broke down.

I'd discovered that he hadn't signed and returned divorce papers to his first wife when we married, meaning he had actually committed bigamy. He seemed to think this was okay because it happened over thirty years ago and his first wife had died five years into our marriage. My trust in him had been shattered, and I walked away. The family home is now up for sale, and he has moved on with his life too. My daughter, Olivia, is happily married and lives in Sunderland with my two beautiful grandchildren.

Glancing over my shoulder, I see Alfie asleep and snoring lightly. I look in the rear-view mirror and smile, thinking of John earlier and how he'd grinned when I told him about this new case in Birtley. His smile had faded a little when I mentioned I'd be staying overnight.

'Aww, no,' he cried. 'But I'll miss you!'

I teased him. 'Get away with you. Work is taking up nearly all of your time at the moment anyway.'

'Yeah,' he'd said, 'but in-between, I know you're here for me to come back to - for one of your earth-shattering kisses and cuddles.'

I'd giggled. 'Well, you can always come and join me for a night if you're missing me that much?'

From the first week I met John, everything between us felt easy. No awkward silences or difficult conversations. We both say what we think and talk issues through together. It's so much more relaxing and mature - I don't have to tread carefully around his self-esteem, unlike with Allan. We are far more suited to each other as a couple than I ever was in my marriage. Some might say John and I are still in our honeymoon period, but I hope not. I know I'll never feel any different about him, and I hope he doesn't either. I squirm in my seat thinking of how good we are together.

The traffic moves, and I drive smoothly across The Tyne Bridge. Even though it's undergoing refurbishment, and John had warned me about possible traffic jams, I carry on, following Doris's instructions up through Gateshead. Leaving behind the busy little town of Low Fell, I slow down, nearing the now-famous,

Angel of the North sculpture. I glance to my left when I see the sign for The Angel View Inn, where I'll be staying tonight.

The big roundabout is busy, and I drive slowly, following the car in front and navigating between lots of red and white cones.

Finally, I'm on my way down the bank into Birtley, and Doris tells me to turn right, which I do, and then right again, where I see the small street sign saying, 'The Hollys.'

I turn into the small estate and when Doris tells me, 'You have reached your final destination,' I pull up outside Karen's house as Alfie stirs on the backseat.

Peering up at the house, I bite my lip. Since moving to South Shields, I've only been involved in a couple of cases assisting a local private investigator.

When I first started, John tried to bolster my confidence. He'd said, 'Look, you're friendly, open, and a good listener, which brings out the best in people - so you'll be fine.'

I remember the two cases I'd helped with - one, where I collated information in a complex criminal case, and another, where I trailed a man whose wife had accused him of having an affair and wanted a divorce. However, that was working alongside a professional. Here in Birtley, I'll be doing it all on my own. Although I've done a little sleuthing before, and Karen does seem desperate for someone to help find her parents, I cringe. Will I be able to do anything for her? Or will I fall flat on my face and humiliate myself?

I remember John's words, shrug my shoulders, and to use one of my mother's expressions, I recite, "Only time will tell, I suppose.'

I grit my teeth, determined to sort this case out then climb out of the car.

CHAPTER TWO
Karen's parents are missing

I look around the houses in front of me as the road in the estate swings around a slight bend. The area has a mix of two- and three-bedroomed detached houses. My first impression is how clean and tidy all the houses appear, with white grille-effect windows and garage doors to the side.

These won't be cheap, I reckon, and smile. A few cars are parked on the driveways, but I figure most people will be at work. However, a black door opens, and I see a lady step out and wave. I decide this must be Karen, and she's been waiting for me to arrive.

Climbing out of the car, I open the back door to unhook Alfie's harness and clip on his lead while Karen walks towards me.

'Hello…' she calls out.

'Hi, Karen,' I reply. 'Am I alright to bring Alfie in? If not, I'll just let him stretch his legs and give him a drink.'

'Oh, yes, that's fine – I love dogs.'

She hurries over, and I shake her hand as she greets me warmly. Alfie hops out of the car to perform his little circular dance that says, *Hey, look at me!*

Karen bends down to stroke his head and ears. 'Oh, isn't he adorable!'

I relax, knowing my beloved dog is having his usual effect on strangers – there aren't many people I've met who don't fuss over him. Alfie had loved John from day one, but for some reason, he'd never been totally at ease with my soon-to-be, ex-husband, Allan.

My dog has a good sense of people, I think, as I follow Karen up the path to her house with Alfie on his lead.

From behind, I can tell Karen is a classy lady just by her clothes. She's wearing a fine-knit black sweater and cream, silky tie-waist slacks that compliment her slight figure. She looks to be around five foot four, with a short blonde bob that swishes as she strides through the hall into an immaculate, large lounge.

'Lets go through to the conservatory, as it's such a lovely day,' she says, leading the way.

Alfie and I follow her into what looks more like a sunroom, though I'll admit I don't know the difference.

'What a lovely room,' I say, watching Karen pull back her shoulders.

'Yes, it is, thanks - now I'll get us a cuppa.'

Karen sails through a side door, obviously into the kitchen. I look around the long rectangular room. Three large rattan chairs face an immaculately trimmed lawn that would rival Allan's garden back in Gosforth. He'd been obsessed with cutting the grass, whereas I've always thought there's more to life than running around with a lawnmower. I smile, thinking of my little flat in South Shields, which doesn't even have a garden.

Alfie tugs at his lead, desperate to get out on the lawn. I whisper, 'Just hang on until Karen comes back.'

I think of her stylish outfit and look down at my M&S yellow daisy dress, which is two summers old now. I sigh and swallow hard, wishing I'd worn something more tailored and professional. Shrugging, I know it's too late to change. However, it does happen to be John's favourite dress; he always says it suits my sometimes madcap nature.

I tap my well-worn flat strappy sandals together and tut at my bright orange nail polish. At the time, I thought it would match my unruly curls, newly highlighted with yellow streaks by the hairdresser. Now, I curl up my toes and think it looks plain silly.

Sweat gathers on my forehead as I sit in one of the big chairs. The sunroom is warm and sultry. I dig into my handbag and pull out two small combs, sliding them into the sides of my hair to lift the curls from my neck and shoulders.

My spirits lift when I notice a small pine table in the corner. On its shelf lies the cover of the first crime novel I wrote years ago. Even after all this time, it still makes me grin to know someone is reading one of my books.

After leaving university, I'd worked in publishing and, over the years, wrote seven crime novels while bringing up my daughter and running the family home. Back then, I was known for my orderliness, with a strict routine and discipline for my writing. The memory gives me a boost, and I lift my chin.

Karen returns with a tray of tea and biscuits, and I sit up straighter.

As she places the tray on top of the table, I say, 'Hey, I see you have one of my novels!'

She nods. 'Yeah, when your niece told our Sam about you, I thought I'd read your book to hear your voice in the story before we met.'

'That's so kind,' I say.

'Not at all. I'm loving the storyline so far. I can tell you have an inquisitive mind.' She bites her lip. 'If Mam were here, I would give her the book next.

She loves reading and goes to the book club at the library every month.'

I blush at the compliment and notice Karen looks upset mentioning her Mam, Violet. She opens the conservatory doors, commenting on the heat. I breathe a sigh of relief as a cool breeze wafts through, knowing it will cool me down. She hands me a mug of tea and glances at Alfie.

She smiles and raises an eyebrow. 'Does he want to go out?'

I nod. 'Well, yes, if it's okay for him to be in your garden,' I laugh. 'He won't dig any holes.'

Karen opens the door, and I let Alfie off his lead. He scoots outside, nose to the grass, sniffing around.

Sipping my tea, I resist the biscuits and figure it's time to get down to business. I start by trying to learn more about this sophisticated woman sitting opposite to me. 'So,' I say, 'maybe you could start by telling me about yourself and the family.'

Her big, worried eyes meet mine. Her carefully pencilled brows furrow, and her expression clouds over – obviously at the thought of her parents.

She nods, swallowing a mouthful of tea. 'Right, well, I've got one son called, Lucca. He's in his first year at York University, reading English and History. He wants to go into law.'

I swivel in my seat as she points to a photograph of him on the wall behind me. Lucca has the same blue eyes as Karen. He's a good-looking lad, and I can tell by the wistful look in her eyes that she adores him. I tell her a little about Olivia and my grandchildren.

She nods. 'I'm divorced now. My husband met a female comedian and moved to Wakefield.

He said the depressing atmosphere of our funeral business was too much. Honestly, I was glad to see the back of him!'

She's got a sense of humour, I think, and can't help but grin. 'Maybe she cheered him up with her jokes and put a smile back on his face.'

Karen shrugs her slim shoulders. 'I haven't heard from him for years. He keeps in touch with Lucca and never sees him short of money - I'll give him that,' she says. 'However, back then, we were in a different place - we started in a terraced flat in Mitchell Street, near our business, but I moved here on my own with Lucca in the millennium.'

We talk about family breakups and I tell Karen about my situation. As we discuss the pros and cons of starting again, we seem to find a sense of solidarity within our conversation. Friendly, but not personal, as if neither of us wants to give away too much. The more we chat, the more I like Karen. I reckon she's in her late forties and her communicational skills, like mine, are second to none. We have much in common, although Olivia is older than Lucca, but I had her when I was eighteen.

Alfie returns, looking up at us beseechingly. I ruffle his head. 'Unless, I'm very much mistaken, Alfie is ready to stretch his legs.'

Karen drains her tea. 'That's fine,' she says. 'Let's walk to the crematorium, then I'll take you to Mam and Dad's house.'

'Great idea,' I say. 'I'll just use your bathroom first?'

Washing my hands, I notice the small bathroom cabinet door is open. Unable to resist, I glance over my shoulder as if someone behind me, and take a peek inside.

I spot expensive face creams and make-up alongside two boxes of co-codamol effervescent tablets. I know these are strong painkillers and remember how my father became addicted to the codeine shortly before he passed.

Of course, Karen could have a genuine medical complaint that warrants them. Still, I lick my dry lips and store this information away in the back of my mind. Is Karen a people-pleaser hiding emotional scars with a dangerous habit? And, of course, reliance on an addictive drug may cause misinterpretation of certain situations.

Or perhaps the tablets have been there unused for years, like much of the clutter in my own bathroom cabinet. Hearing Alfie whining downstairs, I hurry back.

CHAPTER THREE
Long Bank

We leave The Holly's with Alfie trotting between us, cross the road, and head up onto the main street, which Karen tells me is Durham Road. Chatting as we go, Karen points out a few landmarks on the other side of the road: the large Coach & Horses pub and, further down the main street, a sign for the CO-OP's small funeral parlour. It's inside a detached house with blue frames and a conservatory on the side, displaying a sign reading, "Co-operative Memorials" alongside different coloured headstones. Now, that's a conservatory, I think, whereas Karen's is more of a sunroom.

I ask, 'Is that your competition?'

She smiles. 'No, not really. It's a big town now, and there's room for us both. Although there is another new funeral director that has opened further down on the main street amongst the shops, which is a concern to Josh.'

I remember our first telephone conversation and how Josh, her brother, runs their day-to-day funeral business while Karen handles finance and marketing.

Karen walks quickly as we turn down a street called Windsor Road. Her walk is more of a scuttle, and where Alfie is loving this, I'm more of an ambler, concentrating on keeping up with them. Soon, we approach the crematorium, with two light-stone pillars and large green iron gates standing open. We pass through into the remembrance garden.

Karen says, 'During the pandemic, the crematorium was only open for services three days a week.

On other days, services were held in Gateshead at Saltwell Road Crematorium. In fact, about ten years ago, our crematorium was marked for closure, but there was an uproar from the people in Birtley, and it was saved.'

A peaceful serene atmosphere envelops us as we walk along the tree-lined path leading to the crematorium itself. I take out my mobile to snap some photographs.

To the right of the path, the remembrance garden is well tended, with a beautiful small tree in the centre and colourful flowers. A small hut at the front holds the remembrance book for relatives, Karen tells me. This smaller area seems to have much older, flatter headstones compared to the newer ones on the left-hand side of the path.

As we walk more slowly along the path, I notice a larger section with newer glossy black and grey headstones. A couple and their dog wander among them. I feel the pull from Alfie and know his antennae are on red alert as he's spotted the other dog, but I keep him firmly on his short lead.

'I must confess, I know very little about the funeral business and, thankfully, have only had to arrange two in my lifetime - one for my elderly mam, and later the following year, another for my dad.'

She nods, and we continue on the path up towards the crematorium, a red-brick building with grey slate tiles and a brown arched doorway.

'This has been like a second home to me over the years,' Karen says wistfully. 'I know all the staff, old and new, and on many occasions, they've made our job much easier.'

I look around and nod. 'So, there are no services today, then?'

She shakes her head. 'They could have finished for the day,' she says. 'Come on, we'll backtrack and go up to where Mam and Dad live.'

I notice Karen is using present tense while talking about her parents. Perhaps she still believes they are alive and well somewhere. I sigh and let Alfie run on his long lead as we walk back up to the main road and cross over to the bottom of a gently sloping street of houses. I read the sign: Long Bank.

To the right, there's a row of small cottages with a plaque in the pebble-dash reading, "Joseph Hopper, Durham Aged Miners' Homes." I decide this looks like a nice area to live. Facing us, the large three-windowed Coach and Horses pub appears recently painted in grey with a children's play area behind it.

'Is this a popular place to come?' I ask Karen, looking around.

She shrugs. 'It used to be, especially for family lunches on a Sunday, but it changed hands a while back, and I'm not sure how it's doing now.'

We stop at the bottom of the bank, and I look up at a leafy, wide slope lined with detached houses. It's even nicer up here, I think, as we begin walking up slowly. Karen stops outside one of the detached houses.

'This is their house,' she says pensively.

An elderly lady is in the driveway next to the Braithwaite's' house, moving her dustbin out ready for collection.

Karen introduces us. 'This is Daisy Scott, who's lived here as long as Mam and Dad have.'

I smile at the old lady, who has white permed hair and is wearing bright yellow rubber gloves and a flowery housecoat over her fine-knit jumper and skirt. She skilfully manoeuvres her dustbin around a sweeping brush and nods at me.

'Hello, it's nice to meet you.' I say, stepping closer. 'Daisy, can I just ask - when was the last time you saw Violet and Lawrence?'

She purses thin lips and raises an eyebrow. 'Now, let's see,' she says. 'It was about ten days ago, because I was putting the recycling bin out early, just like I am now. We have this once a fortnight, and the general rubbish bin is collected on alternative weeks.'

I smile, knowing I do the same at my flat, although I don't put it out two days early. It's amazing how people judge events by this schedule.

'Doctor Braithwaite had been there, cutting the grass and getting towels in off the line – and then the next day, they were gone!'

I notice how she refers to him as "Doctor" rather than by his forename, but decide this may simply be a mark of respect.

'How strange.'

She nods. 'Yes, it is, because they always tell me when they're going away.'

Out of character, I think, along with everything else Karen has said. 'And the neighbours on the other side of the Braithwaite's?'

'Oh, Brian and Eileen are on a three-month cruise, so they won't have seen them leave in the last two weeks.'

Karen has walked ahead up to the front door with keys in her hand, and Alfie is sitting patiently by her feet. I join them and wave goodbye to Daisy.

Karen says kindly, 'Dad reckons Daisy is going a little doolally in her old age, so I wouldn't put much emphasis on what she says.'

I nod. 'And their car?'

'It's a white Audi A3. Mam doesn't drive, but it's been missing since the day they left -- whenever that was. The police can't trace it either.'

I follow Karen into a large lounge with big windows letting the sunlight stream through. The three-piece suite looks old but of good quality, as do all the furnishings.

'So, just remind me - on the day you discovered them missing, where were you, and what you were doing?'

She nods. 'Well, when I didn't get an answer on the Monday night, I called up here the next morning at 11 a.m. and found the house like this. I knew instantly something was wrong…'

I nod. 'And then what?'

I called Josh and Sam, but neither of them had heard from Mam and Dad either. Josh came straight up, and after numerous calls to their friends with no luck, we contacted the police. They've both got their mobiles, although Dad hardly ever uses his. I even found Mam's old address book and used that to call around.'

Karen glances around the room, her posture stiff as if she still expects to see her parents walk in at any moment. I step forward and squeeze her shoulder gently.

She sighs heavily. 'So no one knows exactly when they disappeared. It could have been Tuesday or early on Wednesday. The police told us there was no sightings of them on any CCTV, even though they've done a sweep of cameras in the area.'

'Standard procedure,' I say, my gaze drifting to a low wooden coffee table in front of the marble fireplace. Two holiday brochures are lying there.

Karen places her hands on her hips. 'The police told us to check out fiends, family, and associates, which we've done. They've uploaded details and photos of Mam and Dad into their national database, but apparently, they rank low on the "risk" register. And, Josh reckons there's hundreds of people reported missing every day so the data base will be swamped with photographs,' she says. 'But I get the feeling the police think they've just gone off for a holiday somewhere.'

I can see the worry on Karen's face, but from the police's perspective the brochures will support that judgement.

'And passports?' I ask.

'They're in the bureau.' Karen walks over to a large rosewood bureau, slides open the top drawer and holds them up.

I nod. 'Karen, remind me – when was the last time you spoke to them?'

'Sunday morning. I popped up for a coffee and everything was normal. Dad was reading the *Sunday Express* and Mam was scuttling around with her coffee pot, opening a packet of ginger biscuits.'

'And then you didn't get an answer to your message the next night?'

She nods miserably. 'That's right.'

'I'm sorry if talking about them is difficult,' I say. 'I just want to get a handle on what's happened.'

'Oh no,' she says quickly. 'I love talking about them – it keeps them close, in a strange sort of way.'

I smile and for the first time I see her eyes glisten with unshed tears. I take her hand so she knows I'm with her. She slumps down into a fireside chair, stroking the blue velour arms.

'I can still see Dad sitting here, grumbling about the Labour councillors with his newspaper. And I keep asking myself - was there something I could've done to stop this from happening?'

Alfie, my loyal sensitive dog, shuffles up to her, placing a paw on her knee as if to say, hey, it's okay, we are here for you. I smile down at him as she strokes his head absently.

She mumbles. 'I'd give anything I own to have them back here again doing their usual things. Mam hurrying in from a bowls match, making tea or baking on a Sunday morning like she's always done.'

The ache in my throat tightens as I look at her. 'This has to be so hard for you all.'

My words sound feeble but I'm floundering not knowing how to console this woman. Since I met Karen she has seemed constraint, hyper organised and in charge of herself but now her vulnerable side is showing it seems worse than having an overly-anxious woman to deal with.

She sighs. 'I was always a daddy's girl. Mam was strict with me growing up. She taught me how to run the funeral business, just like Grannie taught her, and thought it was her duty. But as a teenager, I found it depressing. Dad told me, "Follow Mam for now, and learn the trade. Think of it as an apprenticeship - later in life, you can choose to do something else, but at least you'll have a profession and a salary to fall back on whereas your classmates might not even have a job to go to as a career."'

She glances at a large framed family photograph on the wall – a portrait of the whole family grouped in front of the funeral parlour, taken in the early 90s. Lawrence and Violet are together at the back and the three children in front.

'And he was right – as usual,' she murmurs.

'And Josh? Did she teach him, too?'

'Oh yes, but Josh loved the business from day one. He threw himself into the modern changes and ideas, which lightened the load for me, so to speak.'

I smile, but can't imagine how funeral services could be a chosen career path for anyone. Still, I need to understand the family better.

She continues, 'Where Braithwaite's Funeral Directors was concerned, Mam was serious and driven but she had a wicked sense of humour. Some would call it dark, like most undertakers. They're surrounded with grief and try to find a lightness in tragedy as a release mechanism.'

I've heard similar things from police officers and firefighters. I nod, encouraging her to go on.

'Mam handed the business over to me and Josh when she was fifty-eight and retired. She couldn't keep up with the new changes and it was time for the younger set to take over.'

Karen walks over to the mantle, and a space in a layer of dust where a photograph frame once stood. 'I gave this photo of Mam and Dad to the police.'

She swipes her fingers along the dust and tuts. 'Mam was never the best housekeeper!'

Karen picks up another frame and hands it to me. I take it carefully in a mark of respect for which I'm being trusted. The couple look happily wrapped up in warm jackets with Lawrence's protective arm around his wife. He has gold-rimmed glasses with a thick grey moustache, which I suspect, hides a slight smirk. He has the air of a man whose words carry weight and are totally believable as a doctor.

'Oh, what a lovely photograph of them both.'

Karen smiles fondly. 'Yeah, it was taken about two years ago in Saltwell Park. One of their favourite places to visit.'

I jot the name down in my notebook as she reminisces about childhood firework displays in the park.

We head into the kitchen and I ask, 'Is it okay to take a few photographs as we go – it'll help me build a better picture of them.'

Karen nods, leading me back to the hallway. Another door is firmly closed, and I ask, 'So what's in that room?'

Karen smiles. 'That's Dad's office. It used to be his dispensary and has always been kept locked. The police did look inside and found nothing of interest.'

We mount the stairs with Alfie trotting behind us. I pause at the top of the landing and note the intact locks on the back and front doors. Although I know the police would have taken note of this too. No sign of forced entry which means if there was someone here, Violet or Lawrence had let them inside. My pulse quickens and all my senses are heightened – this is turning into a proper mystery.

. We wander around the two smaller bedrooms and Karen explains which room she slept in with her younger sister, Sam and then points out Josh's bedroom.

She holds open the third door and I follow her inside. 'And, this is Mam and Dad's bedroom.'

Pretty pink rose curtains hang at the window with a big king size bed in the centre. White fitted wardrobes fill the length of one wall with a small dressing table and mirror in the middle. A stool with a pink furry lid fits nicely under the table which has been put into place before leaving.

It is all neat and tidy, unlike my bedroom in the flat, and I wonder if Violet knew she was leaving or was just a naturally fastidious lady. They certainly haven't left this house in a rush and, there's no signs of a robbery gone wrong. Thieves pull out drawers and leave them open so they would have had to drag out this stool to open the slim drawer on top.

Karen says, 'The police took Dad's toothbrush and Mam's hairbrush away in plastic sample bags for DNA, and that's when I was close to tears. It was like something off a TV drama and I couldn't believe we were doing this. Their parting shot was – let us know as soon as they turn up. It's as though they don't believe they're missing?'

Hmm, I think, but ask, 'Is there anything big or small in here which looks different?'

She surveys the room, and shrugs. 'I don't think so,' she says, and then narrows her eyes. 'But hang on a minute something is missing,' she says slowly. 'There was always a small silver frame on the dressing table which Mam loved. It was a smaller image of the large one on the wall in the lounge – that's weird!'

Adrenaline races through me as I know this is significant. It certainty looks as though Violet knew she was leaving. I ask, 'Karen, have a good look around to see if anything else is missing.'

She opens wardrobe doors, flicking through hangers with dresses and jackets. Shoes are neatly placed along the bottom and handbags on a shelf above. I smile to myself wishing my clothes were arranged like this – it would make life much easier, but as with the lawnmower, I've more to do than organise clothes methodically.

'Well, no clothes seem to be missing from Mam's side. She hasn't taken any of her nice going-out clothes,' she says.

I check Lawrence's side and nearly stumble over a pair of highly polished brogues. They are sitting together with toes pointing towards the wardrobe door. Both brown laces are loosened and I can tell these weren't taken off in a hurry.

However, I scribble in my notebook, Lawrence must have been wearing shoes to leave the house, so had he considered wearing them but changed his mind. They look lonely and empty, even sad somehow, as if they weren't good enough for the trip.

Karen glances over my shoulder. She opens his wardrobe door, picks up the shoes and puts them on the bottom with piles of others.

'It looks like he is wearing his usual slacks and pale blue linen jacket because they're not here.

It's easier to see what he was wearing but not so much for Mam because she's got twice as many clothes!'

'And the suitcases?'

'The big black case they usually take on holiday is gone,' she says looking up. 'They usually keep it on top of the wardrobes.'

We head downstairs and Karen turns to me. 'The police have checked their bank statements and credit cards – they've never been used at all. Which is an oddity in itself because like most women, Mam is often shopping and buying stuff behind Dad's back.'

I grin. 'Ah, so a bit of a shopaholic?'

We smile at each other as she nods but I latch onto the words, behind his back and wonder? Do all married women do this? I never did, but some husbands might control the purse strings. Was Violet a browbeaten wife? I also know with missing partners, spouses are considered as suspects but both their parent's are gone, therefore, in this case, it doesn't apply.

Kaen says, 'The police have said their next step is to organise a public appeal on TV. Probably on *Look North* news program which all local people watch, but I haven't heard from them. Although they did say most people take a two week holiday break so they'd do it afterwards if they don't return.'

I scan the coat stand and monks bench by the front door and raise an eyebrow. 'Are there any coats or jackets missing?'

Karen frowns shifting coats aside. 'Mam's grey mack isn't here, so she might have taken that with her.'

I jot this down. We leave, heading back to The Holly's.

My mind races. The missing suitcase, the untouched bank accounts, the missing silver photo frame – something doesn't add up. And I intend to find out what.

CHAPTER FOUR
Karen Braithwaite

Karen rushed through her front door, closed it firmly shut, and stood with her back against it, breathing deeply. She could hear Faye pulling away in her car and thought about the woman she had just met and spent the last hour with. She liked Faye and knew they had much in common, but as usual, she didn't want to encourage a close friendship. After all, this was strictly business.

Karen could tell Faye was a clever lady by the questions she asked and knew she wouldn't miss a trick. That was ideal for finding her parents, but for digging into family problems - well, that was another matter. Karen knew they would have to be careful and choose their words wisely. Her fingers begin to twitch as she thought about the co-codamol tablets. Her shoulders and neck were tense, with a headache forming along her forehead. Probably stress, she thought as she slowly climbed the stairs to the bathroom.

Until her parents went missing, Karen had managed to follow a tapering plan at home by herself, taking the tablets only when absolutely necessary. But all this upheaval had heightened her need for them - or her fix, as she called it.

Addiction at its worst, she thought miserably, pulling out a strip from the box containing two effervescent tablets. She glared at them as if they were to blame for her mam and dad's disappearance.

Thinking back to the previous Sunday when she had visited Long Bank and told Faye that Dad was reading his newspaper, she was no longer sure.

Karen sighed, remembering how she had suffered from a headache that morning because Lucca had had a run-in with his tutor. She had taken co-codamol before leaving her house. Had Dad been there? Or had he been at the swimming pool? She shook her head miserably, knowing the medication might have clouded her thoughts - she simply couldn't remember.

Karen was fully aware of the dangers of painkiller addiction – the damage they could cause to her liver, kidneys, heart, and circulation - but she consoled herself with the same old promise: this will be the last dose, the final time she would weaken and succumb.

It had all started the week Lucca left for university. One of her friends had said, 'It's the empty nest syndrome rearing it's ugly head!'

She had silently scoffed at the idea. Karen had plenty to keep her occupied, running the business and working out at the gym every other day. She had dismissed it as pure nonsense. However, by the end of the following month, when she found herself wandering around the house talking to Lucca as though he was still there, she'd had to admit there was some truth in it. At times, she felt quite desolate.

The racing heartbeat, dry mouth, and sore throat from crying had been frightening. When the constant headaches began, she went to see her dad, in whom she had complete faith. After a diagnosis of possible migraines, he had reassured her. 'There's nothing serious to worry about, Karen.'

Of course, he didn't know by then, she was taking the medication three times a day. At the time, she thought the tablets were wonderful for relieving the headaches, and the codeine made her feel as though she could cope better. They gave her a comforting, floaty feeling, as if they were the answer to all her problems.

She had missed everything about Lucca - his sharp sense of humour, his support within the family, even their arguments about school uniforms and mixing with a bad crowd. Thankfully, that phase hadn't lasted long, and he had distanced himself from them of his own accord. Of course, he had been away on school and scout trips, before, and she had felt hollow pangs until he'd returned, but this was different. This was more than just a pang.

Heading downstairs into the kitchen, she knew, if she was totally honest with herself, these were just excuses. Dropping the tablets into a glass with a few inches of water, she stared out over the garden and felt the loneliness creep around her like a grey cloud on what had been a gloriously sunny day.

Most mothers complain about their children dumping piles of washing when they return home, but Karen longed for Lucca to be here, with or without the numerous pairs of jeans he wore. The kitchen calendar was marked with big red hearts for a weekend in eight weeks when the university holidays began. She prayed he would come home to stay. The longing to see her son, and the constant worry about his safety, was so intense it often manifested as actual chest pain. All she could do was hope he was looking after himself, eating properly, and being sensible at drunken parties.

She had seen news reports about how dangerous the river in York was for students and the fatalities that have occurred. One night, she'd had to switch off the television and ring Lucca just to hear his voice and control her panic attack. She had talked to her dad about her fears, but he had simply said, 'Karen, stop being silly, York is as safe as any other city! He's a sensible lad and, may I add, a good swimmer.'

The thought of Lucca swimming while drunk in the cold, dark river had made her feel physically sick and then reach for the co-codamol.

All her mam had said was, 'It's what is called letting go, Karen.'

She'd wanted to snap back, tell me something I don't know, but she had held her tongue and simply nodded.

However, in her more rational moments, Karen knew it was wrong to wish Lucca was at home. Ultimately, she wanted him to be happy and enjoy his further education without a neurotic mother clinging to his neck. She cringed at her own description, filled with self-loathing.

Karen swirled the dissolving tablets with a spoon and sighed. How had she allowed herself to become so isolated, and end up alone with her false bravado face. It was the face she applied along with her lipstick before facing the public at work, and even with her family and acquaintances.

She had never had close friends since she left school - only what she thought of as local acquaintances. Her two Birtley friends from Lord Lawson Comprehensive had long since drifted away once she started work full-time in the funeral business, and especially after she married. The first five years of her marriage, when Lucca was born, had been her happiest ever.

Now, she thought back to some of Faye's questions and closed her eyes tight shut. What if both her parents were dead? Or one of them was dead and the other was wandering aimlessly lost? With a heavy heart, she knew if one of them was to return home, she could only pray it would be her dad.

She had never been close to her mam. They had never done the usual mother-daughter type of things as Violet had always done those with Sam. Perhaps, Karen thought, as she drank down the dissolved tablets, it had been enough to work with her Mam everyday, so they didn't needed to interact during leisure time. All her life, she'd quite simply been a Daddy's girl, and she choked back a sob, knowing he had to come home.

She wandered through to the lounge and laid her head back onto the sofa, breathing a sigh of relief. Within twenty minutes, the codeine began to take effect, calming her down.

The same friend who mentioned empty nest syndrome had suggested getting a dog for company. After meeting Alfie today - who was adorable - Karen thought it might help. Walking would be more beneficial than driving everywhere, and she remembered how soft and silky his fur had felt as she'd stroked around his ears. She'd had to stop herself from cradling him like a baby. Like Lucca had been.

Of course, she hadn't told Faye about their family issues. Outward appearances were everything to her - and to her dad. He would want Faye to see them all as the perfect, happy family, if there was such a thing. That was the image Karen had tried to uphold.

She closed her eyes and heard Dad's voice: 'Don't worry, because all families have secrets, and ours are no worse than others.'

Unravelling family secrets, of course, would not bother her mam. Karen knew Violet certainly wouldn't loose sleep over disgrace and scandal in the town – unless, of course, it affected the business, which had always been at the top of her list of priorities. In Karen's eyes, her mam had often looked like a trapped bird in a cage, desperate to be free and spread her wings.

40

CHAPTER FIVE
The trail begins in Birtley

Although Karen gave me instructions to go back up to The Angel View Hotel, I enter the post code into my sat nav, knowing that Doris will get me there if I take the wrong turn. Following the car in front around the cones again, I take the third exit off the roundabout, drive up a small slope to the hotel entrance, and park in the main car park.

There seems to be a collection of old, light stone buildings, which I reckon were once barns, renovated from the farm in rural settings. I look up to the red terracotta tiles on the roofs before getting Alfie out from the back seat. In front of me, a small board reading, "Hotel Reception" is fastened to a large black iron gate. We head inside the restaurant and bar. The hotel rooms, with white doors, seem to be on the upper level above the restaurant.

I'm warmly greeted by the staff before being taken further down the drive from the main hotel to what looks like a small cottage, split into two units. The receptionist assures me that this will be ideal for me with Alfie. I open the door to find a cosy lounge, kitchenette, and bedroom with crisp white bed linen and brown soft furnishings. Everything looks spotlessly clean, and I know they're right – this is the perfect set up for us. John will love it too when he joins us tomorrow night.

The lounge is lovely, and I'm glad I decided to stay over rather than drive back and forth every day. Unpacking my holdall, I place the laptop, note book, and pencils onto the coffee table.

I may not be methodical when it comes to cutting grass or storing clothes, but when it comes to writing and work procedures, I am highly organised.

Alfie gulps at his bowl of water while I feed him his last meal of the day. Glancing through the information leaflet in the room, I wander over to the large window with a low brown fence outside. Looking to my right, I see the torso and top of The Angel of the North.

The leaflet states, "The sculpture was made by Anthony Gormley and erected twenty-six years ago. It is seen by one person every second."

I whistle through my teeth in awe, feeling my fingers tingle at the sight before me.

Yesterday, John had said, 'It's now a local identity in Birtley, just down the bank from the Angel. And, I read how Newcastle United football fans once pulled a shirt over the statue when they were drunk.'

I'd laughed at the time, but looking at the Angel's height now, I have no idea how they'd managed to do this.

I think of John beavering away in South Shields police station, gathering information for his criminal investigations. A slight ache fills my chest, knowing he won't be looking forward to going home because I'm not there.

When I first met him, I likened him to Professor T from the television show I'd loved. But once I'd got to know him and scraped away his outer appearance and manner, I reached his underbelly and found one of the kindest, most genuine men I've met. Not that I have met many men, having been married since I was eighteen.

But one of John's main attractions was that he was the total opposite of my then-husband.

Shaking my head, I continue to stare out over the Angel and recall Karen's comments as we walked back to my car. She had given me her view on the sculpture, explaining that many people in Birtley don't like it.

I shrug. Whatever their thoughts, it has certainly put Birtley on the map, attracting thousands of visitors who come to marvel at its enormity. In a whimsical thought, I imagine that beneath the serene span of the Angel's wings lies the gentle slope down into Birtley, as though she is watching over the town, and looking out for its people.

Sitting on the sofa, I start my notes. As I jot down thoughts next to the photographs I've taken, I wonder why, after nine days of their disappearance, the police have nothing.

Karen mentioned a pretty Asian detective who had first visited them - pleasant and understanding but seemingly unconcerned about their missing parent situation. I shake my head slightly, wondering if the police are not taking this case seriously, but know I can ask John's advice later.

My stomach rumbles, so I head over to the restaurant. It's a large room with a polished wooden floor and a mixture of round and rectangle tables, creating a warm, cosy atmosphere. Glass doors lead outside to tables on a paved area, but the sun has gone in, so I decide to stay indoors. It's still early, and there aren't many diners yet, so they allow Alfie to sit under my table. The food is great, and I eat hungrily while thinking about the case.

44

Once Karen had opened up to me, she seemed genuinely grief-stricken in her own way. From the few things she's told me, it's clear to see they are a very close family, their bond strengthened over the years of running the business together.

I think of Violet, the matriarch who built the business while raising her family. How could a mother leave her children, even though they're adults now? According to Karen, her parents are perfectly fit and active. Lawrence swims twice a week, and Violet playing bowls three times a week. I speculate about their mental health – could either of them had problems?

Finishing my meal, I recall last year when I struggled with poor mental health having panic attacks and a racing heartbeat. Thankfully, they're now a thing of the past. My daughter believes it's because I'm happier in my new relationship, and maybe she's right. But no matter how anxious I'd felt back then, I would never have voluntarily left Olivia, even though she's now in her twenties.

Walking back to my room, I think about my own parents when they were in their seventies. How would I have felt if they'd gone missing? Even though I was married with Olivia, I knew how vulnerable they were in retirement, dealing with minor health issues. Dad walked with a stick after a hip replacement, and Mam suffered from asthma and chest conditions.

So, are Violet and Lawrence considered vulnerable because of their ages, despite being in good physical health? I ponder this as I enter my room, make a coffee in the small kitchen, and open my laptop.

Karen, Sam, and Josh have always been close, according to Karen, and they'll be even closer now this has happened. Especially Karen and her younger sister, Sam although I haven't met her or Josh yet.

Karen had said, 'My brother keeps things close to his chest – but men tend to do that, don't they?'

I had simply nodded and smiled, but now I've discovered that it was Josh, not Karen, who filed the missing persons report. That puzzles me, and I scribble a note to myself: Find out where Josh was and what he was doing the last time he saw his parents.

I begin researching online, and find the definition for a missing person is, "anyone whose whereabouts can't be established is considered missing until they are found, and their well-being is established or otherwise confirmed."

I also read that it's a common misconception that must wait 24 hours before reporting someone missing – but you don't. The police emphasise that it's not a waste of time to report someone missing and state they are there to protect us, and our loved ones. When you provide them with information about a missing person they will review and assess then email to confirm that they've got your report and tell you what to expect.

And this, according to Karen is exactly what has happened. I've heard John say many times how the first 24 hours are crucial. I jot this down and note that I need to track the children's whereabouts on the day their parents disappeared. What they did that day and which neighbours they saw, although I have done this myself with Daisy. I also have my copy of the exact photograph Karen gave to the police.

I make index cards for the three children and their parents hoping to fill in these throughout the case. On Karen's card, I jot down my thoughts about her so far, and write, 'She may have an addiction to painkillers.'

Next, I sketch a quick family tree diagram. However, because of Violet and Lawrence's age, both sets of grandparents have long passed but I intend to keep adding to this as I delve further and create a picture of their lives. I trace Violet's family back to Rowlands Gill and Lawrence from Coxhoe, a small village near Durham.

I find how Lawrence had been an only child, therefore, there are no siblings to trace on background searches. I enter both names online and cast my net wider using the information from the missing persons report. Apart from the funeral business there are zero hits, and I decide their disappearance is not a big enough issue to be in newspaper reports after nine days.

I also do a ring-around of local hospitals to check if Violet or Lawrence have been admitted since the police last checked. I speak to admissions and medical record department but there are no records of them anywhere.

Karen had said that Violet's brother worked in a factory in Birtley – Komatsu - which had previously been a Caterpillar tractor factory for years. Her uncle Jack had worked there all his life but died at seventy, being overly fond of a few more tipples than were good for him. However, he always said they were a great company to work for and that the staff were well looked after.

Hoping to put together a picture of the family in Birtley, I trawl public records and text Karen with questions:

Me: 'It says online that The Hub is now closed – is that right?'

Karen: 'Yes, it's a great shame because it was well used by the community.'

Me: 'However, Birtley Community Centre is still open, with warm spaces and free bowls of soup on a Thursday for those in need?'

Karen: 'Yeah, it's near our business, but we've always known it as the Miners' Welfare Hall. It's a huge old hall with a balcony, stage, and an amazing ornate staircase. I think it's nearly a hundred years old now.'

Me: 'And the bowling green – is that still used?'

Karen: 'Of course, that's where Mam plays three times a week with her friends.'

Me: 'It says that Birtley Medical Group is the only surgery in Birtley?'

Karen: 'Yes, that's where Dad spent his working life – it's at the bottom of Harras Bank.'

I nod at all her answers, knowing in the morning, I'll find these places when I look around the town on my own.

Me: 'And can I meet up with Josh tomorrow afternoon?'

CHAPTER SIX
The Belgian's have been in Birtley

The next morning, as I walk out onto the roadside, deciding to leave the car behind, I look at the Angel in her full glory and spot a gathering of people underneath the huge iron feet, taking photographs. There's a brown coffee station van in the car park where visitors are ordering drinks.

Following the pedestrian diversion signs with Alfie trotting along beside me, I walk down into Birtley, talking to him all the while. I've often wondered what other people think of me chatting to my dog all of the time and decide they'll probably think I'm a little unbalanced. But, in all fairness, I've seen other dog owners do it too.

Alfie is three years old now. When we brought him back from the shelter, Allan had said he needed a name. I nodded and started going through male names in my mind. The TV was on in the background, playing a quiz show, and the question was to name a 1960s film staring Michael Caine. I'd called out, 'Alfie!' Our new Spaniel had lifted his ears and looked straight up at me. And that had been it - Alfie was his chosen name. So much so that I couldn't think of him as anything else now. He sort of grew into his name.

***

I've always thought it best to talk to people face to face rather than on the telephone so I can gauge their reactions. I begin at Birtley Community Pool, where Lawrence used to swim twice a week. I tie Alfie's lead to a handrail outside the main doors, where I can see him through the glass window, and whisper, 'I'll be two minutes.'

While waiting to talk to the young girl at the reception desk, I overhear a man in front of me explaining how Gateshead Council closed the pool last year. However, the townsfolk launched a crowdfunding scheme to get it up and running again. He also mentions how Prince William came to officially open the pool, although this had been kept top secret for security reasons. He winks at me while checking in for his swim, and I thank him for the information.

I glance through the glass window at the side of the desk and see the tempting water in the pool, glistening under the sunlight streaming through a skylight. Hmm, I think, I wish I'd brought my swimming costume.

I feel a fluttering in my stomach, knowing I'm at the beginning of the trail to find Violet and Lawrence, and I hope I can uncover details that may help Karen's family.

The girl at the desk, with long blue hair, looks up at me, and I smile, holding out the photograph of Violet and Lawrence in my hand.

Passing it to her, I say, 'Can I ask if you know this man?'

She squints at it and nods. 'Oh yes, that's Doctor Braitwaite. We all tease him by calling him Mr Grump because he's always moaning about something.'

I chortle, and then, laughing, she continues, 'He has a monthly subscription card and comes a few times each week. Although, come to think of it, I haven't seen him this week at all – maybe he's on holiday?'

Slipping the photo back into my bag, I compliment her on her blue hair colour and watch her preen, twisting a long strand around her short, stubby finger. 'Oh, thanks! I had it done for my 21st birthday party at the weekend.'

I grin. 'Ah, twenty-one years, eh? Well, I hope you have a great time.'

Hoping I have her on my side a little, I ask, 'Would it be possible to check your computer and see exactly when his last visit was?'

Her slanted grey eyes flick down as she presses a few keys. Leaning forward, she whispers, 'Yeah, it was Friday the 13th'

Unlucky for some, my superstitious mind notes, and I remember this date realising he was here just a few days before they disappeared. From the corner of my eye, I see two small children approach Alfie. I thank her, then hurry back out through the side door.

Alfie is performing his tricks for the kids, who giggle. I untie him, and we walk back down the path while I'm deep in thought. If Lawrence and Violet had planned a surprise trip away, as the police seem to think, would he have gone swimming just two days beforehand? Of course, if they'd been taken against their will, this swimming session would have been part of his normal weekly routine.

***

Just down from the pool is the doctor's surgery on the bottom of Harras Bank. I pop inside, although I suspect the police would have already been to his place of work. I discover that the receptionist has only worked there for six months and doesn't know Doctor Braithwaite. However, on the way out through the glass doors, I spot a middle-aged lady in a cleaner's tabard with a mop in her hand. I ask her about Lawrence.

'Oh yeah, he looked after me from when I was a little girl and was lovely. But, I have to say, in the few years before he retired, it was as though he couldn't be bothered with my ailments and lost all of his friendly manner. He told me once he couldn't wait to retire.'

I nod, taking in this information. 'I see. I suppose doctors are under a lot of pressure nowadays, and he could have been longing to finish work, as many older people do?'

She shrugs. 'Maybe, but he was quite short and abrupt with me and other staff in the surgery, so I don't think he left under a good cloud,' she says, before brightening. 'However, I've got a lovely female doctor now.'

I bid her goodbye, noting that's two groups of people who haven't a good word to say about him. I begin building a picture of his character.

***

Crossing the road, I stand in front of the Komatsu factory and remember Karen's brother. A group of workmen sit outside on the wall in their overalls, having lunch with Greggs pasties and sandwiches. My stomach rumbles, and I head into Greggs for one of their famous sausage rolls, feeding a little of the sausage meat to Alfie, who licks his lips.

The front street shops are similar to those in any other town centre: a garage, Savers, a butcher's, a computer shop, hairdressers, nail bars, barbers, cafés, a travel agent, and a large care home called Covent House. Karen mentioned that rates and rents are really high now, leading to many shops opening and closing in rapid succession.

On the other side of the road, I spot a small restaurant called, Aioli. Although it's mid-morning, I see a tall man with a black ponytail and a beard inside. I open the door, and he greets me warmly. Deciding this would be ideal for John and me to have a meal tonight, I ask if there's a table free.

He grins. 'You're in luck - I've just had a cancellation for our first sitting at 6 pm.'

I glance over the menu and smile. 'Perfect,' I say, giving him my mobile number for confirmation.

***

I decide now to focus on Violet now and see what I can find out about her in town... Heading into Morrison's supermarket opposite, I sit down at a table in the corner of the café. Alfie slopes under the table on the brown wooden floor, resting his head on his paws. I'd love a coffee and, as I'm deciding how to order it, two elderly ladies sitting at the next table look across.

The oldest lady, who I figure is in her nineties, calls over. 'Just leave him there under the table, and we'll keep an eye out while you get your drink.'

I thank her and return from the counter, which is covered with clean white subway tiles, with a latte in my hand. I've never been inside a Morrison's café before and am impressed with the selection of food and drinks on offer. It's a nice, light and bright room with grey wooden chairs and spotless pine table tops. I sip the strong, hot coffee with satisfaction.

The elderly lady, dressed in a blue skirt and top and wearing a delightful white sunhat, leans across to me and asks, 'Are you new to Birtley?'

Grateful for the conversation, I nod and smile at her friendly tone. 'Yes, it's the first time I've been here – I'm helping out a friend.'

This, I figure, isn't too much of a white lie because, although Karen isn't a friend yet, she is an acquaintance.

'Ah, that's nice,' she says and points to the other woman, who looks a little younger. 'We meet in here after our session with the Birtley Heritage Group.'

Hoping to find out more about the town and funeral business, I decide to keep the conversation going. 'That's interesting,' I say. 'Can you tell me a little about Birtley?'

The younger lady says, 'Well, our Mary here is the best person to tell you about old Birtley because she's been here all her life, and is ninety-two now!'

Mary smiles coquettishly, her bright hazel eyes twinkling at the comment, and pulls back her shoulders. 'Well, Birtley is in a dip below the higher A1 road, which saved us from the German Luftwaffe during the war. At the time, to the right of the high street, alongside the terraced houses of Mitchell and Jones Streets, was the big Royal Ordinance Factory, which we always called the ROF. This was where ammunition was made, but the clever men in charge painted the flat roof green so that, from above, it look like a field. Apparently, the Luftwaffe circled and circled in their Messerschmitt planes, desperate to bomb the factory, but this clever deception saved the town and all of us from death and destruction.'

I've always loved history and am transfixed by Mary's story. I lean in closer. 'Oh, wow! And were you all scared?'

A melancholy look fills her face. 'Well, I was only seven when the war started, so I didn't really understand,' she says. 'My mam wouldn't let me and my brother go to the air-raid shelter, so she pushed us under the table, away from the window in our flat. But the following year, we used to look up at the plane lights in the dark sky with the whirling, screeching noise.'

The younger lady leans further across. 'Of course, now the factory has been flattened to build new houses. But our heritage group, based in the library, has published a book called *Who Were The Birtley Belgians?* which we're really proud of.'

'That sounds great. I might stop in at the library and buy a copy,' I say. 'And what have Belgians to do with Birtley?'

She nods. 'Thanks for that. The book tells the story of how, in WW1, our government commissioned two factories in Birtley: one to produce shells and another, ran by local women, to produce cartridge cases. An agreement between Britain and Belgium brought six thousand Belgians here over two years with the necessary skills in armament manufacturing. By 1918, they'd made two million shells, making Birtley one of the most productive sites in the country.'

I whistle through my teeth in awe. 'Oh wow, that's fantastic! And where did they live?'

'Well, a unique self-sufficient village was built, named Elisabethville after the Belgian queen. They had their own traditions and customs and were housed in workmen's cottages laid out in rows with two and three bedrooms and gardens.'

I sit back and grin. 'Hey, what a story – no wonder you want to tell everyone about it.'

Mary says, 'And the women in the cartridge factory even had their own football team!'

Bubbles of laughter form in my stomach, and I chuckle. 'Hey, I bet the England Lionesses would love to know about that!'

The two women chat between themselves now, and I look from one to another. They're animated, and I can see how enthused they are talking about their town and their book.

The younger lady says, 'The village was enclosed with an iron fence and had its own church, food store, shops, post office, and cemetery.'

My ears prick up with at this word. 'Oh really? And where was the cemetery - is it near the one that's there now?'

I figure when I visit Josh in the funeral parlour, I can ask him about this. They give me directions, which I scribble down. Remembering how Karen had told me about Violet going to the book club, I mention this and how she is now missing.

Mary tuts. 'Yes, we've all heard about their disappearance. Mrs Braithwaite is a nice woman. I remember years ago when she did my mother's funeral – it was a lovely service,' she says. 'It's shocking2, but I did notice the last time I saw Violet that she was very quiet and seemed distracted.'

I make a mental note of this information and see Alfie getting restless under the table. Pushing back my chair, I thank them both and get up. They wave, and I leave them to their conversation.

Karen had given me a card from a hairdresser's called Hair Flair, where Violet went for a cut and colour and her nails done meticulously every fortnight. I step inside the shop and show the photograph to the lady at the reception desk. She checks on her computer and tells me Violet missed her last appointment, which wasn't like her.

I sigh at this news and wonder - had Violet simply forgotten? I know if I had a holiday planned, I'd certainly want my hair and nails done beforehand, so why hadn't Volet? The lady asks if I want to book Violet in for another appointment, but I shake my head and leave the shop.

***

As the sun is still out, I decide to keep walking along the high street before going to see Josh. Passing by the library on the right side of the road, I pop inside. Karen had mentioned that her mam often read two books a week.

Looking around, the library feels fresh and possibly newly painted. I head up a few steps to the counter and sigh with pleasure at the sight of shelf upon shelf of books. Hmm, I think, my idea of heaven. In the past, libraries always had a certain atmosphere - traditional rules, hushed tones, and the slightly musty smell of old books. Readers would whisper and keep to themselves enjoying their own space and quiet time.

However, libraries have always provided an invaluable free resource to the public, and nowadays , they feel more engaging, with authors giving talks about their books and exhibitions showcasing local history.

A middle-aged man at the counter greets me, and I buy a copy of the *Birtley Belgians* book, knowing John will enjoy reading it too – he, like me, is a history buff.

I show the librarian my photo and ask if he's seen Violet recently.

'No, I haven't seen Mrs Braithwaite for a few weeks now,' he says.

He smiles and clicks onto her account in the computer. 'In fact, the books she borrowed last month are due back tomorrow.'

I nod. 'Right, thanks, I'll let her daughter know - I'm sure she'll sort them out if they're at Violet's house.'

***

As I continue walking further up Durham Road, I wonder if Violet has taken the books with her – wherever she might be. Talking to Karen on my mobile, I can tell she still believes they are alive somewhere. I sigh. Who am I to dispel her hope? All I know is that, she'll be in for a hell of a shock if they aren't.

To my left is the fire station, next to another care home called Lindisfarne, and I'm reminded of last summer when John and I visited Holy Island for the weekend. The memory makes me smile, and I marvel at how often the name is used in the North East. It had been my first time staying by the sea, and at first, I wasn't sure about moving to South Shields. I've always been more of a countryside person, but within a month of sitting on the beach with Alfie while John was on his paddleboard, I began to enjoy people watching on the sand and letting the world go by.

Now, I love living by the coast and appreciate how lucky Alfie and I are to be there.

It's certainly very different to living in a town. Of course, it gets busy with holidaymakers in the summer, but they bring a lively, seaside vibe and it's good to see the town bustling and making much-needed revenue.

***

Further up the road, I stop outside tall green iron railings and look across at the white octagonal pergola in the centre. There's a sign on the side of a green wooden planter, with bowling balls on each corner – how cute, I think. I read the words: Welcome to Birtley Town Community Bowling Club.

This must be where Viollet plays, I reckon. I spot two women walking around the neatly cut grass. One of them approaches, and I show her the photo.

'Yeah, I'm on Violet's bowling team, and I know her closest friend, Sheila. She texted and rang Violet when she didn't turn up for their last game. It's not like her to let the team down.'

Once again, I hear what a lovely woman Violet is and how the whole town is unsettled by her disappearance.

I leave the bowling green and cut down Edward Road, thinking that, unless I've caught the people of Birtley on a particularly good day, they all seem very friendly. There's a warm, welcoming feeling in this small town, unless, of course, I'm missing something?

CHAPTER SEVEN
Josh in the funeral business

Walking down to the funeral business, I remember Karen's words about Josh's wife, Alice, and how they live in a big house behind the funeral parlour with their two fostered daughters. I'm already impressed by this and reckon that any couple willing to foster or adopt children must have big hearts.

I approach the business and read the Braithwaite signage, knowing I've found the right place. I smile in satisfaction at their window and overall appearance. Where other funeral parlour windows often display examples of headstones, this one is entirely different. The main window has a beautiful arrangement of seasonal flowers in two large vases, with summer blooms evident—dahlias, marigolds, and two tall sunflowers. A clear and well-presented price list is encased in a simple yet classy frame, a reassuring sign for anyone considering entering the premises.

***

Opening the door, I step into a small reception area painted in a soft cream shade. The cosy space is furnished with two- and three-seater beige sofas, creating a relaxed atmosphere. Behind a small desk, a leather easy chair sits in front of a computer screen, with an arrangement of thank-you cards pinned to a noticeboard. Josh is seated there, but as soon as he sees me, he jumps up and hurries around to greet me, shaking my hand warmly.

'And you must be Faye Chambers?'

No need for introductions here, I think. 'Is it okay to bring Alfie inside?' I ask.

Josh's smile turns into a playful grin. 'Oh, yessss,' he says, dropping to his knees to ruffle Alfie's ears and head. 'Hello, little man,' he whispers, and Alfie practically glues himself to Josh's long legs.

I reckon this man must be at least six foot three or four, as thin as he is tall. An image of him dressed in an old-fashioned black funeral director's attire, like something out of *Oliver*, makes me smile.

Josh jumps up and gestures towards one of the sofas. 'Please, Faye, take a seat.'

I do so and immediately recognise the same features in his face as Karen's, especially their eyes. It's obvious to anyone that they're siblings.

A door in the corner opens, and a small woman walks towards me with an outstretched hand. 'Hello, Faye, I'm Alice,' she says.

'It's so nice to meet you both,' I reply. 'And are you responsible for the beautiful display of flowers in the window?'

Alice blushes to the roots of her short black fringe and nods. She is the complete opposite of Josh—only around five feet tall and as short and round as he is tall and thin.

'Yes,' she says. 'I did a flower-arranging session at the WI in Chester-le-Street and thought the display would brighten the window. People passing often pop in to say how much they like the arrangements, and I change the flowers with the seasons.'

Alfie settles by Josh's feet as he continues to ruffle his ears, and I sink back into the cosy sofa while Alice disappears to make tea.

Knowing I need answers, I decide to find out more about Josh's background in the business.

Karen told me he's a couple of years younger than her, making him forty-six, but he looks much younger.

'So, Josh, how long have you been working here?'

He explains, 'Well, since school really, when I started helping Mam and learning the ropes, as it were. Our Karen was already working here, but since she was better at maths, she took on all the finance and marketing.'

I smile. 'And did it make a difference when your mam retired from the business?'

He nods. 'Oh, yes, but in a good way. Mam loved the freedom when she first left. Karen and I thought she'd be calling in all the time, trying to organise us and check what we were doing, but she didn't. She simply told us this was her time to do as she pleased. With her bus pass, she travelled around the area, especially South Shields and Whitley Bay, where she walked on the beach for hours while Dad was still working.'

'Good for her,' I say.

'Yeah, it was.'

Alice returns with a tray of mugs and biscuits, placing it on the coffee table while moving aside an open brochure showing different examples of coffins—some in willow wood, others in cardboard, with or without lids. On the front is an American-style casket, available to order from a special website. A shiver runs up my spine as I realise I'm about to learn exactly what happens in places like these.

I sip my hot tea while Alice chatters about the warm weather. She's wearing cute knee-length pink shorts and a T-shirt.

'I came back on the train from Glasgow the day after Violet and Lawrence went missing.'

I'm not great with accents, but I'd recognised the strong Glaswegian twang as opposed to the softer Edinburgh enunciation when she first spoke. I let her continue.

She shrugs. 'I'd only been up at my parents' with our two girls for three days when I had to return, which interrupted our holiday plans.'

'That's a shame,' I say before turning to Josh. 'And you weren't with them in Scotland?'

I already know he wasn't, but I want to hear their version of events, so I play dumb. He shakes his head while Alice continues.

'No, I like to go up on my own because I love visiting them. Even after fifteen years down here, I still miss my home city and get homesick. We lived in Pollokshields, which was a lovely area to grow up in, and I spent hours at the Kelvingrove Art Gallery. Have you been to Glasgow before?'

I shake my head, but she continues before I can answer.

'Oh, that's a shame—you must go! The gallery is still free to enter and is built from gorgeous rose-coloured stone from Dumfriesshire. Inside, there's the famous painting *Christ of St John of the Cross* by Salvador Dalí.'

She stops for breath, her big blue eyes wistful. 'I go to see it every time I visit, revelling in its glory time and time again. Have you seen it?'

I shake my head and answer quickly this time. 'No, but I'll definitely put that on my bucket list.'

She beams. 'And there's an amazing cathedral with the Necropolis built up on high ground, offering stunning views over the city.'

I smile again, realising she's giving me a guided tour of Glasgow. But upon reflection, I figure she's simply proud of her home and heritage. The Scots are a noble nation, but I need to steer the conversation back to us.

Josh dunks a biscuit into his tea and muses, 'We are all shaped by where we're born, where we grow up, and where we live. My grandparents ran this funeral home for years, with Grandma as the patron, and then my own mam took over.'

Alice drains her tea, then excuses herself to make the children's tea. I give a small sigh of relief.

I turn to Josh. 'I must admit, I know nothing about the funeral business.'

He stands up and gestures around the room. 'Oh, right, well, I can show you around and explain, if you'd like?'

I smile at his enthusiasm, but a niggle forms in the back of my mind. Unlike Karen, whose face twists in agony when she talks about their parents, Josh seems almost indifferent to their disappearance. Is this a non-grieving son I'm talking to?

'Come on,' he says. 'I'll show you around the place.'

I take a deep breath and follow him through the side door, leaving Alfie snoozing under the table.

And I follow him through the side door, past their viewing room.

He explains, 'We respect the person's customised last wishes to the letter, and relatives often want their favourite keepsakes in coffins, like T-shirts, helmets, and teddy bears. They also like their favourite flowers in wreaths of all shapes and sizes,' he says. 'Joanne's Florists on the High Street does a great job arranging wreaths, and we work together on special requests.'

We enter the next room along the corridor, which is larger and very cold. I shiver. Big drawers line one wall, with stainless steel tables pushed into the corner. Thankfully, I sigh, the room is empty.

He continues, 'This is where we receive the bodies, but we never work alone and always supervise each other. As well as Karen, we have two more staff members who have worked here for years alongside us. We collect bodies from the morgues in hospitals in our van, where the gurney has security belts for transport. Upon arrival, we transfer them into these drawers in the refrigerated storage unit and log the paperwork from the hospital mortuary. We carry out the embalming process in this prep room.'

I stand behind him, staring at his grey trousers and blue shirt, not wanting to look around in case I see something I don't want lingering in my mind afterwards.

'Of course, Mam taught me and Karen, but since then, we've been on more up-to-date courses to learn newer, more streamlined techniques. And of course, all the solutions have changed.'

He taps the outer drawer in front of us. 'This is Mr Smith, who has just arrived from the morgue, and his daughter has brought us his army uniform, which the family want him to wear. So we'll be dressing him in the morning.'

I hold my breath, praying he won't pull out the drawer. My heart begins to beat faster, and my palms sweat. I know I've written about dead bodies in my crime books, but until last year in South Shields, I had never actually seen one. My stomach knots. However, Josh doesn't open the drawer but instead explains how they dress people.

'It can be tricky dressing a corpse, and we often split the back of a jacket to make pushing the arms into the sleeves easier once they've come out of the fridge. We'll probably roll Mr Smith onto one side, tuck in, and then repeat from the other side. The limbs—especially on a big, overweight man—can be very heavy to move, so we tuck the shirt behind his back and neck while doing up the buttons and easing the legs into the trousers. I often put the tie around my own neck to make sure I've got the knot right before putting it around Mr Smith. I enjoy this bit—smoothing out the creases in the shirt. Polished shoes and socks can often be awkward, especially if the feet have become misshapen in death. Sometimes we don't bother with shoes unless the family specifically requests them.'

Josh has moved back towards the door again, and I follow him, glad that we are leaving the room, although I have learned about the process and the family business.

Walking back along the corridor, he says, 'With the women, our Karen still likes to do their make-up from photographs of how they looked before they passed. My sister is very capable and attentive to the tiniest details, and she reckons the intimate act of applying foundation to someone's face gives them a healthy colour so they're fit to be viewed by the family.

When the family arrive tomorrow, our Mr Smith will look a whole lot healthier than he does now.'

I hear Alfie whine as we enter the reception once more. I tell Josh about the women in Morrison's and ask for directions to the Belgian section of the cemetery.

He nods. 'Look, I've nothing much on for the rest of the afternoon, so I'll walk you around there.'

***

Within minutes of being back outside in the sun, I warm up again and walk leisurely next to Josh, who saunters along the road. Considering his long legs, he's an ambler, like my John.

He talks as we walk, and I learn how they first began fostering children and how, so far, they have devoted their lives to the kids in their care.

He whispers, 'Don't tell Alice I've said this, but I wish every child could be my own—though I'd never admit it to her because it's her infertility that prevents us from having babies. In my eyes, family is everything, especially now that Mam and Dad have gone missing.'

He kicks at a pebble as we reach the lower area of the crematorium, and I figure he's a man who bottles up his emotions—probably why I initially thought he wasn't very upset about his parents being missing.

He points out where the factories had been, now demolished, and then says, 'At first, I was distraught with worry about them both when they went missing. But, as with most things, life goes on. I knew Mam would want me to keep the business going, as we had funerals booked, and the last thing she'd want would be for us to let people down.'

We reach a memorial in the Belgian area, which Josh tells me is from the War Graves Commission, commemorating thirteen Belgian soldiers who died while living in Elisabethville. Then he points out one of the Belgian headstones, engraved with a diagram of the Belgian flag.

'Of course, most relatives mark the anniversaries of their loss each year, and these memorials often include angels and wings. We work closely with our churches in Birtley too. There's our Methodist Chapel on Station Lane, which has just celebrated 100 years since opening. There are some great black-and-white photographs in the library of how it was built—twelve men holding trowels and saws, with makeshift scaffolding. Amazing,' he chuckles. 'There was no such thing as health and safety at work back then!'

I hear the pride in his voice for the town and smile.

With his parents in mind, I ask the main question. 'So, when was the last time you saw Violet and Lawrence, and where?'

We sit down on one of the benches, and I pull out my notebook to record the details. 'Can you remember your conversation? I mean, did they seem upset? Worried? Sad?'

Josh shrugs, reflecting. 'They were just normal. We'd all been up late on Sunday morning because Mam has always baked. When we were kids, she made all our favourites—chocolate cake, apple pie—and she still does the same now. Her cheese scones are legendary. Even now, she makes a Sunday lunch if they're not away for the weekend in the country. Our girls have always loved going, as did Karen's son, Lucca.'

I grin. 'Now, cheese scones would be worth a visit.'

A wistful look crosses his face as he leans forward, his long fingers trembling. He clasps his hands together. 'Yeah, they both loved to drive out for pub lunches in the countryside—either Rowlands Gill, where Mam was born, or up to Northumberland. Hexham, Alnwick, and another firm favourite, Morpeth.'

I jot this down and ask, 'Did either of your parents use social media?'

'You're joking, aren't you? Dad calls it pointless trash and always says, "Why waste time on that when you can read a good book?" He has never sent a text in his life. Another of his phrases is that Mam's mobile is glued to her hand!'

Remembering Karen's comments about Violet hiding shopping behind Lawrence's back, I wonder—is his dad a controlling man?

Josh continues to reminisce. 'Dad is a great man. Years ago, he chucked out the stabilisers from my bike and shouted, "You don't need them—just ride the blooming bike!" But looking back, I see he knew everything. I spent years trying to please him. Even now, he's my rock. I go to him with every issue I have, and he always has an answer. But as a man? I couldn't say I like him much. He's everything I'm not—bombastic and terse. Though Karen reckons he has a softer side, I've never seen it.'

I look at Josh and think of my own dad.

Josh suddenly grins. 'Alice thinks they were taken against their will—kidnapped!' He snorts. 'And I said, "So where's the bloody ransom note, then?"'

Trying to lighten the conversation, I joke, 'Maybe she's been watching too many reruns of *Taggart*?'

He grins, relaxing. 'So, Faye, what the hell has happened to them?'

I pat his arm and shake my head. 'Well, that's something I'm going to try and find out.'

CHAPTER EIGHT
Josh Braithwaite

Josh is back in the office of the funeral parlour, sorting out paperwork from the filing cabinet. It's not his favourite job, but he grits his teeth, knowing it has to be done - or Karen will be on his back about their tax records. How she finds this part of the business interesting, he'll never know.

However, as Alice often says, 'Just be glad you don't have to do her bit as well, because then you'll have something else to moan about!'

Josh sighs. Was he becoming a miserable man who constantly complained about his lot in life? He shakes his head and consoles himself with the fact that it's simply because his parents are missing, and everything seems to be getting on top of him. Even Alice, in her softer moments, agrees - it's not an easy situation to deal with.

Thinking back to the last hour he spent with Faye makes him smile. She's a nice woman, he thinks, and they got along well together. When Karen had told him how Faye, a budding amateur sleuth, was coming to see if she could do to help, he'd been sceptical. What could a sleuth do that the police couldn't? But, as usual, Karen had made her decision, so he went along with it. That's just the way they were, he supposed.

Shrugging, Josh repeats the words to himself: *his parents were missing*. He had been asking himself how this could happen, hour after hour, since the day they disappeared, and still, he has no answer.

He slumps back in his office chair and kicks the filing cabinet drawer shut with his shoe. What if he never saw his mam again? His insides quiver, and his throat tightens. He knows he couldn't bear the pain if she didn't come home to them all. He has always loved her beyond reason. She could do no wrong, and if anyone harmed her, he would kill them - and willingly do time for the crime.

Josh shakes his head, knowing his next thought was an awful thing to admit, but he did it anyway. If something had happened to his dad and he never came home, it wouldn't be the end of his world. He would miss him, of course, but at least it would put an end to the pointless, lifelong effort to please him. From being a little boy, he had strived for his dad's approval and praise, which never came. His father's absence would finally put those feeling to rest.

That wasn't the image he'd painted for Faye. He had always told little white lies - or at least, that's how he justified them - to prevent upset. Some people might say they were great whopping lies, and a way to crave his dad's attention, but Josh had never believed in psychology – it took too much time to think.

He had told Faye the story about the stabilisers on his bike but omitted the truth: how his Dad had smacked his ear in temper and how it had stung for hours afterwards. Josh had been used to his dad's shouting, but that had been the first time he'd actually lashed out. That day marked the first time Josh had felt afraid of him.

The argument afterwards between his mam and dad had been loud and ferocious. Josh had hidden under his quilt, shaking with dread about what might happen next.

Some of his friends at school had divorced parents, and he didn't want that. If it happened, everyone - especially Karen - would blame him.

Josh shakes his head at the memories and thinks back to when he was sixteen. He had taken the key off the hook in the kitchen and crept into his dad's office. At that time, he'd been desperate to find a reason why his dad seemed to dislike him and treat him so coldly. But he found nothing. There were no personal items in the desk drawers - not even a diary. The only thing he had discovered was paperwork from a court case in which his dad had testified about a suspicious death. The rest had been all medical documents, which he couldn't be bothered to read.

Karen had always been their dad's favourite. She was more like him - confident, self-assured, an organiser. Whereas, he was none of these things.

His mam often said, 'But you have other qualities to be proud of that Karen doesn't possess, Josh. She doesn't have your kind, thoughtful generosity – you'd never see Karen fostering children like you have!'

Which was true, he thought. But why didn't Dad think like that? Why wasn't Dad proud of their efforts with underprivileged children? He was a doctor, full of sympathy and virtue towards his patients, so why wasn't he pleased that they were giving children a good home?

Sighing, he knew the answer deep down. It was because they weren't Braithwaite children. And, of course, Karen didn't have to foster children because she'd given birth to Lucca - a true Braithwaite. She had given their father a grandson he worshipped. Grimacing, Josh remembers how his dad had taken Lucca to rugby matches at

Kingston Park in Newcastle and taught him to play chess. Josh raged, why couldn't he have done things like that with me when I was a boy?

He'd once overheard his dad moaning to his mam, 'Josh is always hiding behind your skirts - stop mollycoddling him, or he'll grow up like a wimp!'

So maybe, Josh thought, that's exactly what he had become – a wimp.

Josh sighs and looks to the window at the new arrangement of flowers Alice had put together yesterday. He smiles. Aside from his mam, she has always has been the one constant in his life. They'd met in Newcastle one night when he was out on a stag do with his friends.

Alice had been with her own friends from Glasgow, staying in a hotel for a hen party. He had known within hours of meeting her that she was *the one*. He adored her - mainly because she accepted him just the way he was from the outset.

He rubs his chin now. She doesn't know about the lies he's told the family regarding their infertility. Sweat gathers along the collar of his shirt as he thinks of this untruth - and the other lies he's told. His cheeks flush, and he shakes his head, unsure why he does this? But in his defence, he has justified the previous lies as a way to protect others from distress and arguments, which he couldn't cope with.

However, this time, the lie was to hide the fact that, as other men say, *he fires blanks*. Josh couldn't bear telling his dad it was his fault they couldn't have children because it would be yet another failure on his long list. So, had lied and blamed Alice. If she ever found out, it would be like pressing the self-destruct button.

Within six months of marriage, Alice had said, 'Until I get pregnant, how about we foster a child? There's so many children in dire circumstances, and I know we could give one a good family home for a while.'

He had readily agreed, thinking of it as a short-term arrangement. At that stage, it had never entered his mind that the issue might be his and knew Alice thought the blame was hers. Shortly after their application was approved, a seven-year-old boy called Alex arrived. From the first day, Josh had been determined to give him the best childhood possible. He didn't want Alex to be treated the way his dad had treated him.

He had loved Alex and wished he had been their son. He'd played football with him, taken him to see the Tall Ships on the River Tyne, and to the cricket ground in Chester-Le-Street. That day, he'd told Alex the history of the six-hundred-year-old Lumley Castle, and Alex had been enthralled. It was everything Josh had wished his own dad had done with him - but never had. Even now, years after Alex had left, Josh still thought about him – it had been a big wrench.

Of course, he liked the two little girls they fostered now, but somehow, it wasn't the same. Alice did all the girly things with them, though they tried to have at least one family day a week.

With the windows being open, Josh hears the girls giggling coming back from school outside their front door. It cheers him. Shaking off his gloomy thoughts, he strides outside to call hello.

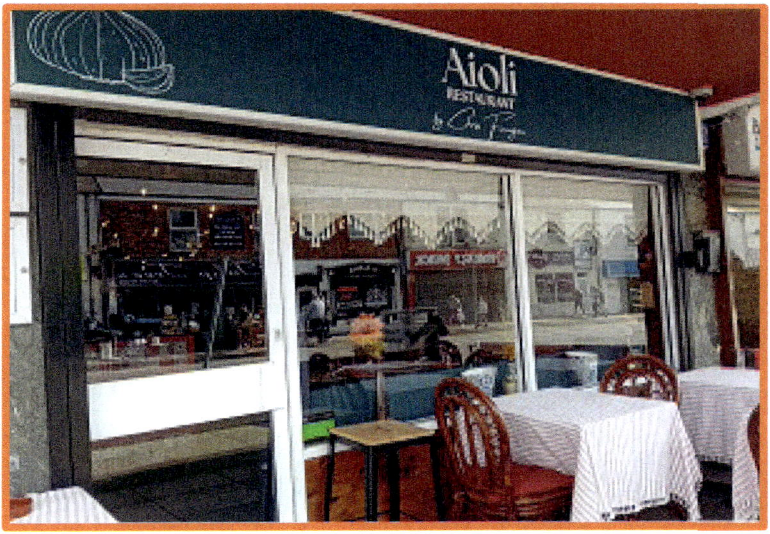
Aioli
RESTAURANT

CHAPTER NINE
Good food in Birtley at The Alioli restaurant

I'm back in the hotel, getting ready for John, who is driving over to Birtley to stay the night. I change into a plain green dress and flat pumps for dinner in the restaurant, then stare closely at my face in the mirror. Taming my big, curly hair, which is cut into a longish bob, has been a lifetime's challenge. Back in the 80s, when big permed hair was all the rage, I'd never had to visit the hairdresser – mine was natural. Now, in an effort to hide the ever-advancing grey, I use a light blonde colour. Finding two sparkly, bling slides, I push them into the curls.

In my teens, Mam had cruelly said, 'You'll never be pretty or girlish, but you can make the best of what God gave you.'

I'd never been quite sure what she meant by this, but I do know God gave me the ability to write and use my brain instead of relying upon good looks. I apply a beige lipstick and examine my big teeth for lunchtime remnants of salad, which makes the dimple in my cheek stand out more. A stroke of dark pencil over my bushy eyebrows and a thin line of eyeliner to accentuate my pale blue eyes completes the look for the evening. Thinking of Mam's past comments, I do know my eyes are my one and only redeeming feature and pull back my shoulders .

A tinkle on my phone lets me know I've received a text message, and I see my friend Penny's name on the screen. Thiis makes me smile and I read, **'Hey there, how are you doing in Birtley?'**

I text back: 'I'm fine, and the case is going okay, but I'm missing John more than I thought possible!'

Smiling, I leave a red heart emoji at the end of my message, knowing she'll understand. Penny lives in Yarm, and we are the closest friends from schooldays. We always called each other besties, with her as the leader and me following her around like a lap dog. She played the celebrity glamour puss, and I, the sedate assistant. However, I was brighter at academic classes whereas she excelled in all sports and, of course, gained an A* in boys and relationships without commitment. Even now, she is still sporty, running every morning and playing tennis and golf at home.

Penny left Newcastle after we finished college and moved to Middlesborough. Although I haven't seen her for a while, we talk at least twice a week and text each other practically every day. She's always been the closest thing I have to a sister, and I love her dearly.

I read her next message and grin. 'Don't worry, Faye, you'll soon be back with him, tumbling in those sheets. You know the saying - absence makes the heart grow fonder!'

I send a laughing emoji and drag my mind back to the case.

Over by the table in the corner of the lounge are my index cards, which I've stuck to the wall with Blu Tack. Removing the card for Josh, I scribble down my notes and, in bold, write: Josh hides his feelings and emotions behind his work.

In other cases, I've used social media to help trace people on Facebook, Instagram, and X by looking at photographs, comments, posts, and likes from friends and strangers who may have connections. However, I sigh – since Violet and Lawrence don't use any of these platforms there's little point.

I know all three siblings will react differently, as will friends and neighbours, but so far, I'm forming a good picture together in my mind of Lawrence and Violet's characters, their lifestyles, both past and present.

I hear John's car pull up outside on the gravel driveway, and Alfie shoots to the door, barking wildly. It amazes me how he always knows it is John and how delighted he is to see him. During the first two years of Alfie's life, living in Gosforth with me and my husband, I can't recall my lovely dog ever greeting Allan in the same way. He'd hardly raise his head and ears when Allan arrived home. Good judge of character, I muse and whisper, 'I know, Alfie, I can't wait to see him either!'

Alfie never moves from John's side when we are all together, and I know John makes him feel safe and secure. Just as he does me.

At the end of our case together in South Shields last year, I'd wanted to take things further with John. We'd gone from meaningful glances to staring into each other's eyes, to him placing his hand on the small of my back when walking together, to linking arms, and then, when I left the guest house, a kiss. That kiss had left my head spinning, and I knew I wanted more.

However, John had insisted, 'Go home and sort out your marriage, Faye. If you want to stay with Allan, then so be it, but if not, I'll be here waiting for you.'

And, that's what I did. I stayed for six weeks, talking everyday with Allan about our relationship, but I knew I'd never trust him again.

We both agreed that we had drifted apart over the last few years, and I admitted that I wanted to be with John.

I'd told Olivia, 'Even if I hadn't met John, I still wouldn't want to stay with your dad.'

She hadn't tried to persuade me otherwise but simply said, 'I just want you to be happy, Mam, and you're not with Dad. Don't stay at home just to keep the family together. I've got my own family now – so go and start anew.'

My gorgeous police inspector steps through the door, drops a holdall to the carpet, and throws his arms around me, nuzzling his face into my hair.

'Missed you,' he murmurs.

Same here,' I say, pulling away from him. Alfie has fastened himself to John's right leg, and John automatically bends over and fusses him. The hairs on my arms stand up as desire races through my body, but I keep it in check until later in the night.

I'd told John on a text that Alioli is a small restaurant and that we'll have to leave Alfie here. While John changes his shirt, I feed Alfie and snuggle him down wrapped in a blanket. 'We'll be two hours max,' I tell him, and he looks at me with huge, soulful eyes that tug at my insides. It reminds me of when I had to leave Olivia with a babysitter for nights out and never felt settled again until I was back home with her.

***

John drives us into Birtley town and parks in Morrison's car park, where we stroll across the road and enter the restaurant just before six. We are greeted warmly by the same man I'd spoken to earlier and we find out that he is indeed the chef, Chris Finnegan.

Chris is from Birtley and spent twenty years working in some of the UK's top award-winning hotels and restaurants until 2022, when he undertook the challenge of appearing on *MasterChef: The Professionals,* making it as far as the semi-finals.

There are only ten tables, with a long leather seating couch on the right-hand side of the room and a tiled floor. The walls are painted plain cream, adorned with select food photographs in gold frames. On the left-hand side is a large cooking area with a counter, allowing customers to watch Chris cook – it's a delight in itself.

From Sunday roasts to a tasting menu with Spanish influences, there's plenty for John and me to choose from. With soft drinks in hand, we order our food while Chris talks with customers, creating a cosy and relaxed ambience.

John leans forward over the table, and with a certain look in his eyes, I know he wants to talk about my case. 'You know, it's hard to disappear and stay hidden these days, with the internet and CCTV on most streets in towns and villages,' he says. 'And you'd need a good memory to stick to a new story and lifestyle - especially at their age.'

I nod in appreciation of his comments, although I had figured that out for myself.

He continues, 'They'd need impressive levels of planning and discipline in a voluntary disappearance, but I suppose the father, being a retired doctor, would be more than capable of this. And what about the mother?'

'Well,' I say, 'so far, she seems the friendly, lovable matriarch of the family but may well be controlled by him.'

I tell him my thoughts about Birtley, Violet, Lawrence, the case so far, including Karen and Josh's characters.

'Therefore, you are down to involuntary disappearance or blackmail? Do you think they are dead?'

I shrug. 'Well, it's been nine days now, so it's not looking good, is it? The police have nothing, and I'm wondering if this is because it's an unusual case and not run of the mill.'

A second opinion from him is the best I could ever have, being a detective in the force, although he doesn't override my cases. He has a way of teasing my way of thinking until I come to the right - or sometimes, the same - opinion as him. Which invariably is correct. He's been at this game an awful lot longer than I have, so I respect his experience and judgement.

Our main course arrives, and I cut into the roast chicken, which is cooked to perfection, as is the sauce and vegetables. I swoon at the flavours, and John joins me with his first forkful of seabass.

'This is probably the best seabass I've ever tasted,' he says, offering me a mouthful to try. I nod in agreement and return the compliment with a slice of my chicken. I watch him enjoying his meal while thinking about him.

John is quietly spoken in company but opens up so much more when we are together. He's invariably clean shaven, which shows off his determined jaw, set in an effort to see a sense of justice in all he does. He has to do the right thing at all costs, and it's one of the many things I love about him. And although I've never told him this, I find his air of authority and the stillness in his manner quite a turn-on.

His interviewing techniques are second to none, as he listens carefully to people, often with a clipped tone in his voice and abrupt responses, until he forms a judgment about them. I remember him in the South Shields case last year, talking to holidaymakers in the guest house, and how his thin lips moved as he drew heavy eyebrows together and sat with arms folded over his chest.

I clear my plate, which is whisked away by the waitress, and tell him about my experience today in the embalming room. 'So, I'd thought it would be dark, smelly, and kind of spooky, but it's not. It was very clean and sterile, like I think an operating theatre would be, although I could see how much care and attention the dead people received from the Braithwaite's.'

The apple tart Tatin arrives with ginger ice cream, which literally melts in my mouth. I turn around and compliment Chris, who grins while telling me it's all in the variety of apples he chooses.

John and I share the desert, and then I sit back in my chair, feeling totally satisfied. I continue, 'And John, there was a leaflet about Pure Cremation, which I figure sounds okay if you don't want all of the razzamatazz?'

'I've got one,' he says.

'Really?'

'Yeah, apparently, they collect you in a solid coffin from anywhere in the UK to a crematorium of their choice and then hand-deliver my ashes to anyone that wants them,' he says, and winks. 'And as my parents are long gone and I've no family, I reckoned Pure Cremation is the most suitable for me.'

A heavy feeling fills my stomach, and it's not from the food. 'Okay,' I say. 'I'm surprised because I haven't got anything in place, thinking I'm too young. However, I do need to think about Olivia and my grandchildren, plus check the upcoming divorce settlement with Allan. I wonder if he has made arrangements for the family?'

John nods. 'Best to find out, and I figured in my line of business you never know what might happen, so mine is all sorted.'

'What do you mean, you never know what's going to happen?'

'Well, I could go into a routine-looking domestic, which years ago wouldn't have been an issue, but nowadays there's drugs, knives, and guns to deal with, and one swift stab in the back....'

He hasn't finished the sentence, but I know what he means, and I'm choked at the very thought of this. I swallow a massive lump in the back of my throat as he asks for the bill.

Why has his dangerous job never entered my head before now? I'd always thought, because he spends most of his time in the office as an inspector, in comparison to the police officers on the beat, that he wouldn't encounter as many dangerous scenarios. However, he probably has more to worry about because he wouldn't get involved with minor cases, only the serious assault cases, which are worse.

My knees feel wobbly, and I hold back the tears which want to escape. I take a deep breath and will myself to park these thoughts and not spoil the evening, but I know it is something we need to talk about at a later date.

Maybe he can see my face betray worry and concern because he changes the conversation. 'We can boost up Chris's reviews because I'm very impressed with this delicious food.'

***

Returning to the car park, John looks around the street. 'You know, I have been through Birtley before,' he says. 'It was on my way to Chester-le-Street to watch the test cricket. It's an amazing place right in front of Lumley Castle – a magnificent backdrop, especially when the flood lights are full beam. I'll take you one day.'

Back in the room with Alfie at his heels, John looks over to The Angel of the North and says, 'Hey, it would make a great front cover for a book – you could call it, 'She's No Angel?'

I laugh and then pull him through into the bedroom, remembering our first night together and how scared I'd been. It had been in his house in South Shields on the first night I officially left Allan. I'd never been with another man, and John also admitted that he was nervous, as it had been years since his divorce. But we fitted together like a jigsaw puzzle and scoffed at each other afterwards for being nervous.

When John has shown me just how much he missed me, we lie propped up in bed looking at the Birtley Belgian book together. The old photographs are amazing, and we discuss the logistics of setting up a whole new housing area within a small town.

I mutter, 'Nowadays, this probably couldn't or wouldn't be done because of planning permissions and legal immigration rules.'

There's no answer from him, and I see his eyes have closed. I lean over him, turn out the bedside light, and snuggle in behind him.

CHAPTER TEN
Lawrence Braithwaite

Lawrence looks around his room in the house - half office, half dispensary - as he quietly reflected on his position and what he is about to do. He had these last ten minutes before they left, with no intention of ever returning. His legs and arms are heavy, weighed down by an unnatural stillness that had settled around him. He knew that Violet would say, 'You've got that pensive expression on your face again.'

When they'd first moved onto the Long Bank, he had nabbed the largest downstairs room for himself, insisting over the years that it remain child-free. The old key hung in the kitchen cupboard. It had always been strictly out of bounds to the rest of the family because of the dispensary, which held drugs, lotions, and potions. Of course, nowadays, prescriptions were only written and given to patients at the surgery, but in what he liked to think of as the good old days, this was commonplace. It was the only space he thought of as his own sanctuary.

He ran his hands over the old wooden desk with its well-worn green felt in the centre, which had once held a blotter when he used an ink pen. He sighed; that was many moons ago. The striped wallpaper was dated and scruffy in places.

A few years ago, Violet had said, 'I wish you'd let me decorate that room - it's years out of date!'

He had grumbled and shaken his head in defiance because he liked his room the way it was.

On the right side of the room was his dispensary, housed in a huge wood case with four glass doors.

The bottles were all brown glass, some still sealed with old cork stoppers, and there were small glass containers holding tablets. Nowadays, everything was plastic, recyclable, without a glass bottle in sight. The whole lot should be dumped, he thought, but had it really been that long since he'd had a clear out? He remembered chucking out the old green ribbed bottles that had once held poisons, but exactly when, he wasn't sure. This was part of his past, and he couldn't bear to look at empty shelves - it would remind him of a career gone by.

Closing his eyes, he remembered Karen's friend at school, Jane, who had fallen on broken milk bottles in a crate. Jane's mam had rushed her to Lawrence at home, where he'd sat the little girl on their dining table and put two stitches in her knee. Chuckling, he thought of GPs doing that nowadays which would be unthinkable. Some days, you couldn't even get an appointment.

The changes in the NHS over the last five years had set his teeth on edge with frustration and temper. So many changes, yet little notice was taken of the medical staff who actually knew where the money should be spent. But he sighed – he no longer had the energy for it.

Everyone had expected him to work past retirement age of sixty-seven, but many had been astounded when he left the very day he got his state pension. 'I've had more than enough and can't to leave the modern-day health service far behind me, he had declared. 'But what will you do with your time?' they had asked. He had thought long and hard about that.

His job at the surgery had always busy, and with the funeral business, they'd never been able to book a two-week summer holiday abroad.

Not that either of them had wanted to lie on a beach sunbathing, but Lawrence had always wanted to travel, and see some sights.

Now, he thought of his family with a grave expression. Lawrence knew that when they left, it would be Karen who would take charge and look for them, which didn't seem fair. Yet, she was the one most like him: hardworking, a no-nonsense work ethic, gumption and fortitude. Not his son, whom he freely admitted had been a bitter disappointment.

Violet had said, 'Oh, but Josh is just sensitive and quiet. There's nothing wrong with that, is there?'

But Lawrence saw it as weakness, a lack of stamina. He knew for a fact that when they did leave, Josh would hide behind his wife's skirts and be an emotional wreck. Josh had married Alice, who was everything he wasn't. Even though her Glaswegian accent grated on him, she was strong and resilient - more like Karen, whom Josh had leaned on since he was born.

He tutted, his mouth twisting grimly at his son's behaviour. These weren't the actions of a decent man. He had found Josh's medical records and knew his sperm count was virtually non-existent, yet he had told Violet, 'Unfortunately, Mam, the blame lies with Alice for our infertility.'

Lawrence had wanted to challenge Josh but, as usual, had bowed to Violet's insistence not to interfere.

His thoughts turned to his youngest now – poor, scatty Sam, a nervous shell of a girl with mental instability. He'd never been able to fathom where she came from. She was nothing like any member of the family, past or present. For nineteen years, he had tried to like his youngest daughter but, for some reason, he simply couldn't. He knew it was a failure on his part and consoled himself with the thought that she had been a late baby, unplanned and unexpected, when really they shouldn't have had any more children. Too old to play games or endure her temper tantrums and clinginess, he found it easier to distance himself from the girl and leave her upbringing to Violet. It wasn't something to be proud of, he thought grimly, but it had been easier to immerse himself in work and ignore her.

As their mother, Violet always devoted herself to the weakest in the family, because he couldn't. In that way, they made a good team. Lawrence knew it was the funeral business profits that had bought their detached house and lifestyle, not his GP salary. Yet, he'd always felt second place to the business. He also knew Violet's pecking order: the business first, then Sam, Josh, Karen, and lastly, himself. This, he accepted as his lot in life. Many other men would consider him a fortunate man.

It was around the retirement age that he first noticed the changes. Violet had left the funeral business to the kids, saying, 'I'm like your father – I've had enough of working.'

But then things began to shift. The cups in the kitchen were put in different places. He couldn't remember if he had if he had moved them or if Violet had. And yes, they'd had a kitchen re-fit about ten years ago but all cutlery, china, baking tins were still in the same cupboards.

The constant repetition of questions about their daily routines drove him mad. He hadn't been able to fathom this - it had been the next sign to say that thought processes had changed. He reassured himself that perhaps it was just a sign of old age as they reached their seventies.

They had not waited long for an appointment. Lawrence knew a few strings had been pulled, and he'd been grateful. But the CT scan showed degeneration - vascular dementia. His knees had felt weak, dizziness overwhelming him as he thought of their time to come and what lay ahead: suffering year by year, humiliation, and all dignity stripped away. This fear turned to anger and frustration. Why did this have to happen? And to his family? Couldn't it have been someone else's?

Fury surged through him, and he banged his fist on the desk, sending two pens rolling onto the floor. Dark imaginings filled his mind. A long tortuous end. He scrambled to the dispensary cupboard, scanning the rows of bottles. Screwing up his eyes, he read the old labels, handwritten in ink. He picked out a large bottle – something resembling chloroform. Did it have a use-by date? He wasn't sure, but he slipped it into the side of his battered-leather doctor's bag.

He then checked the cupboard next to the mini-fridge, finding a small cool bag Karen had once bought him for his sandwiches. It would do the trick. Sliding a thin square box from the fridge, he placed it into the cool bag and then into his doctor's bag. His preparations were complete - he was now ready to leave.

Taking one last look around the room, he rubbed his jaw and quietly recited the doctor's oath. He knew it off by heart.

I shall never intentionally cause harm to my patients, and will have the utmost respect for human life.

I will practice medicine with integrity, humility, honesty and compassion. I recognise that the practice of medicine is a privilege with which comes considerable responsibility and I will not abuse my position.

But Lawrence knew full well - he was about to wield the power of life or death.

92

CHAPTER ELEVEN
Were they spotted in Saltwell Park Towers?

I drive along Durham Road, following Doris's sat nav instructions through the small town of Low Fell. Apparently, the town was named after a water well, and, there's a popular Little Theatre here with progressive players. Doris tells me to turn left down the bank to Saltwell Park, which I do, pulling into the car park. Smiling, I know Alfie will be welcome here, but I do keep him on a firm lead until I get my bearings.

With the photograph in my hand, I look at the background with the huge house and then stand before the real thing, in awe of its spectacular construction. The entire house is built from dark red and yellow bricks, with asymmetrical towers, tall chimney stacks, and corner turrets. The Victorian mansion, designed in the Gothic Revivalist style, is a breathtaking sight.

I take photographs with my mobile to show John. He'll love to see this, I think, grinning. In our day-to-day lives at the coast, we tend to stay within our own little area, but I'm beginning to realise how much more there is to explore in the surrounding parts of the North East.

I check my notes and recall how Karen mentioned that this was one of her parents' favourite places to visit when she gave me the photograph. Violet loves the ducks and wildlife, while Lawrence is fascinated by the history of the towers and house.

A small plaque detailing the house's history catches my eye, and I read with interest. Apparently, it was once owned by William Wailes, a leading stained-glass manufacturer. He had Saltwell Towers built as his family home but later sold it to Gateshead Corporation to be used as a public park. At that time, many local people lived in cramped, dirty conditions, with no sanitation. Diseases such as cholera and diphtheria were rife. The Park provided a "green lung" for local folk to improve their health and opened to the public in 1876 as "The People's Park." It was an immediate success.

By the pull on his lead, I know Alfie is eager to head off around the park and lake, but I hold him back. 'Later,' I whisper. 'I need to go inside the café first.'

Before entering the tearoom, I show the photograph to a couple of ground staff wandering around the side of the house. I don't hold out much hope that they'll remember this couple among the hundreds of visitors who use the park ever day. And I'm right - they have nothing to report. With a heavy sigh. I realise this could be another dead end, but I furrow my brow and chant to myself, Don't give up.

***

Pushing open the door to the Bewick's tearoom, I look around at the large windows with cream blinds and the terrace overlooking the gardens. Square Formica tables and chairs fill the bright, airy, and clean room. A range of sandwiches and cakes is on display, and there's even a puppuccino for Alfie, which sounds inviting. He is busy surveying the floor with his big black nose to the ground, taking in all the new scents. I smile, feeling my spirits lift, and ruffle his ears, knowing he's thoroughly enjoying the adventure.

I love places which cater for dogs - it makes life so much easier - although I understand the rules and regulations of food establishments.

Thankfully, Alfie is now trained to perfection. When I first got him, I attended a dog training group in Northumberland for six weeks, which gave us the fundamentals. That was essentially how my little dog-sitting business began in Gosforth - first with a request from an elderly neighbour to walk her dog after an operation left her with limited mobility. She recommended me to her friends, and within weeks, I had a regular clientele of six dogs on various days to walk. Since moving to South Shields, though, dog walking has taken a back seat as I focus on my new path into amateur sleuthing.

The middle-aged lady behind the counter smiles and I take out the photograph once more from my bag.

'Hello,' I say, 'Can I have a coffee and puppuccino for my dog, please?'

Being short in stature, she grins and peers over the counter top. Her long black hair is scraped back into a ponytail, making her face appear severe, but her big, gentle eyes more than make up for this as she looks lovingly down at Alfie. I nod, recognising another dog lover.

'Take a seat, and I'll bring it over to you,' she says. 'It's quiet today.'

I gather that she's not supposed to bring drinks to the tables, but I do as she bids. There aren't many people around, and Alfie slinks under the table before lapping up his puppuccino. When she places down my coffee, I chat to the lady and show her the photograph.

She nods. 'Oh yes, I know this couple – they come quite regularly,' she says. 'And I'm sure they were here last Saturday because it was the day after my holidays.'

My mouth dries a little as I lean forward and feel my heart rate increase. 'Really?' I ask. 'Are you sure?'

I pull out my notebook, scribble the date down, and calculate that it was five days ago. I want to record exactly what she says.

'Yes, I remember because they ordered their usual,' she says, and pauses while concentrating. 'Yes, definitely. One tea, one coffee, egg and tomato sandwiches, and lemon cake. But we didn't have any lemon, so they both had a slice of coffee cake instead.'

Thank goodness for the elderly who are creatures of habit and know exactly what they like. It has made them easier to track. When you've had a good experience somewhere it gives us an expectation of repeating the same. It would be the same for John and me if we returned to Alioli, hoping the food will be just as good as last time.

'I suppose they were disappointed when you had no lemon cake?' I ask.

'Yeah,' she says. 'But they both enjoyed the coffee cake, and the woman even joked that it was so good she wanted the recipe. And that's how I remember them being here.'

My mind is buzzing now with the first recent sighting! I want to whoop with joy and can almost hear my mother saying, 'Oh, ye of little faith.'

Remembering their car is a white Audi, I ask, 'Do you know if there's CCTV here in the park?'

She raises an eyebrow, and I silently say a prayer. It would be great to get an image with concrete evidence to say they were definitely here with a date and time.

'I'm not sure,' she replies. 'But I think the CCTV is through body cameras worn by enforcement staff . Maybe if you ring the main Gateshead Council number, someone will be able to help you.'

I thank her as she hurries back to the counter to serve an elderly man.

***

It's my first tangible lead - at least I know that last Saturday, they were still alive and here in the Park. Humming a little tune, I head back to the car. Once Alfie is fastened into the back seat, I tap the rhythm on the steering wheel, give a throaty laugh, and shout, 'Yes, yes, yes!' into the car space. Finally I'm getting somewhere.

I know there's little point in asking the staff here for CCTV recordings - it needs to be done through proper channels. Starting the ignition, I bite my lip. Should I tell Karen? It'll raise her hopes, and I suppose it could come to nothing. Who's to say the lady in the tearoom is right, and although she seems certain, she could be mistaken.

I text John, asking how to request CCTV footage in the park from enforcement staff. He replies, saying the police can request it and that Karen will need to call the officer in charge of their case.

I take a deep breath and send Karen a text. 'Can I call in to see you and touch base?'

Karen replies, 'Oh, that's good timing - our Sam is here, and you can meet her too.'

I pull out of the car park and head back to Birtley. I'd rather tell Karen in person than over the phone and decide to play down the sighting - just in case it's a mistake.

This case is certainly testing my skills, I think as the mysterious disappearance unfolds. And it dispels the police's theory that they are off on a long holiday. They were still here just five days ago. But where were they staying last Saturday? And, more to the point, where are they now?

CHAPTER TWELVE
Sam and her partner, Ellie arrive

I pull up outside Karen's house and park behind her car. Before I get the chance to knock, the door swings open, and Karen ushers us inside. While I follow her into the lounge, she calls over her shoulder, 'I'm so pleased you sent the message because our Sam is looking forward to meeting you.'

The two young women sitting on a chair by the fireplace look to be in their early thirties. Quickly, I do the maths and reckon there's at least a ten-year gap between Josh and Sam. A late baby for Violet, I decide and smile at them both.

Karen introduces Sam, who stands up, grinning at Alfie. She makes a beeline for him, but he cowers behind my legs for some reason, wary of her. 'It's okay,' I say. 'He's a little shy with strangers, but give him a few moments and he'll come around.'

I perch on the edge of the sofa with Alfie beside my leg. This, of course, isn't true but it's enough to make Sam slump back down into the squashy brown velour chair.

She nods. 'A bit like me, then.'

From what I can see, there's no resemblance to Karen or her brother whatsoever. Around five foot nine, with bright red hair and a chunky figure, she's wearing scruffy trainers and a black bomber jacket with a heavy rock image on her T-Shirt.

'How's Zoe doing?' Sam asks. 'Although we chat on Facebook, I've not seen much of her since university.'

I look in her chocolate-brown, small eyes and very pale skin. She wears long hoops earrings and has a ring in the side of her button nose. Her fingernails are bitten down, and I wonder if they're always like this or if it's the stress from her parents being missing. Hoping to relax her a little, I tell her about Zoe and my family.

Sam says, 'Well, I have no input in our family business because I don't know how to talk to people like Karen and Josh do.'

A slight ache forms in my throat as I look at Sam, who seems an outsider in her own family, and is clearly very shy. She doesn't take after Karen, with her outgoing personality, or Josh, with his mild, bubbly character.

Ellie sits on the arm of Sam's chair, stroking her shoulder. Ellie looks even more unusual, though I figure this judgement is from my older perspective. To younger people in society, their appearance might be entirely ordinary.

I watch Sam take a deep breath. 'M…Mam doesn't know I'm gay, but our Karen does,' she says, glancing at her sister. 'I loved art and swimming at school but hated everything else. So now, I've immersed myself in photography – mainly black-and-white photos of architecture and design.'

Sam clenches her bird-like hands into fists, opening and closing them as her fingers tremble. She rocks slightly as she talks, and I hope I'm not making her more uncomfortable.

Karen nods. 'Our Sam is really very good but has no confidence and won't assert herself enough to show her work in a portfolio. She mainly does wedding and baby photos to help towards her keep in the flat,' she says, then smiles at Sam. 'And she's always talking about shutter speeds and different lens on her camera, which we know nothing about, but she certainly knows what she's doing.'

Sam pulls back her shoulders slightly after Karen's pep-talk and leans further into the chair, making Ellie shuffle around. They tend to touch each other's hands and arms a lot – it's obviously a comfort to Sam.

I look at Ellie, who has a snake tattoo trailing from her neck down into her shoulder, visible through the gypsy top she wears with a flowing hippy-style skirt. Her slanted eyes, framed by a purple two-tone fringe and streaks in her long blonde hair, give her a sly look. A scowl lingers on her face, as though she's not enjoying being here.

Ellie says, 'And I have a flat in Heaton, which my parents pay for so I can design my own greeting cards which I sell at craft fairs.'

Her voice is clipped, and for some reason, I don't take to her. I feel her staring at me as though weighing me up – just as I am her. She holds Sam's hand and strokes it possessively, as if to say, Sam belongs to me. Or is she simply being protective towards her partner? Perhaps, she's jealous of this family's tight-knit bond?

Sam says, 'Mam thinks Ellie is just my friend and would be horrified to know I'm gay, especially after what I put her through during my teens and at school. She'd never understand,' she says, looking down at her trainers. 'You know, I've always hated my name, and everyone calls me, Sam. But knowing I'll never hear anyone call me Samantha ever again is sad because only Mam did that!'

My heart goes out to this young woman, struggling with her identity on top of her parents being missing. 'But society has changed so much – I'm sure she would be okay with this,' I say, looking to Karen for confirmation.

Karen soothes, 'You're just the same as everyone else who is in love, and I've told you before, it wouldn't matter to Mam.'

Sam shrugs. 'It started at school. I knew I was different because I wasn't drooling over boys,' she wails. 'Then the bullies started with their jibes, so I figured if I could be funny, they'd leave me alone – and it worked to some extent…'

From what I can see, this younger sister doesn't seem to have any perseverance and strength of character that Karen does, but perhaps this could be because of her age. Clearly, she's the baby of the family and may have been mollycoddled all of her life.

I nod and ask, 'So, Sam, when was the last time you saw your parents?'

She tilts her head and grimaces as if completing a difficult task. 'I'm not sure,' she says, looking to Karen for the answer.

I whip out my notebook to record date, time and conversation. 'Can you remember if they were upset? worried? or sad?'

'Well, Mam always answers my WhatsApp messages straight away so I knew something was wrong when she didn't.' Her eyes mist over. 'She sends me silly photographs of things she's seen - furry animals, insects, kids misbehaving - and we giggle at the images.'

'And your dad?'

'You know, I can't even remember the last time I saw him.'

Karen intervenes. 'Wasn't it the weekend before, when you called into mine on my birthday, and we walked up to see them?'

Sam nods. 'Oh, yes. He was in his office for most of the time but called goodbye when we left.'

I work out the date quickly and nod. 'And he was his usual self?'

'Yeah. Being the youngest, Dad always seemed like an old man - forever grumpy and telling me off,' she says. 'Especially when I'd catch him staring at me.'

Ellie snorts, and I watch Sam pick at the skin on her thumb. Is this at the mention of Lawrence? Are there underlying tensions here? My suspicious mind wonders - was it just that they didn't get along, or is there a deeper history between Sam and her dad that only they know about?

My thoughts are interrupted by the front door opening and a male voice shouting hello. Alfie scoots to the lounge door as Josh bounds into the room, bending his tall frame to fuss over my dog. Josh heads over to Sam and - bends down, rubbing his forehead on hers, and then does the same with Karen. I figure this is their sibling greeting, something they've probably done since childhood. Greeting Ellie and inquiring after her health, he receives a nod in reply and sits on the other side of the sofa to me, holding Alfie's head between his knees and whispering to him.

Karen asks him, 'So, how did the service this morning go?'

'Fine, it was a humanist service using a wicker eco-coffin,' he says. 'Along with his favourite song from Coldplay and loads of Sunderland football club shirts with photos.'

I look at Karen, and she explains, 'A humanist service is a non-religious one. There are no hymns, and the coffin is a biodegradable basket.'

I nod. 'Oh, right, thanks. So, nothing like my parents' funerals, which were full of old people wearing black veils, upholding old traditions. I think we even had the obligatory ham sandwiches where everyone stood around looking sad and mournful.'

Josh shakes his head. 'There aren't many funerals like that nowadays; those tend to be for older people. And undertakers are very different too,' he says. 'In Mediaeval times, the first funeral undertakers were woodworkers – typically furniture makers or carpenters – who had the skills required to make a coffin.'

Sam giggles. 'I can't see you making a wood coffin!'

Josh grins and I see silent looks between the siblings. Karen's mouth is twitching as though she's trying not to laugh. I can tell something funny is about to happen, or they're about to share a humorous incident from the past. I look from one to another.

He says, 'Yesterday, I found this crazy website in America with jolly names for funeral businesses. The first one was "Go as You Please" and another, "Burns Funeral Business," he says, chortling. 'And the last one is called, "Am I gone!"

We all laugh, apart from Ellie, who still has the permanent scowl on her face.

Karen grins. 'Oh, really? Wouldn't you have to change the name of the business from Burns, even if it is the family name? I know Dad would – he'd be mortified!'

Sam laughs loudly, nodding her head, and Alfie wanders over to her for a pet. She snuggles her face into his ears.

Josh chortles. 'And can you remember the burial where the hole hadn't been dug large enough for the coffin? Mam hooted about that for weeks…'

I realise now that, together, they are reminiscing about their mam and dad within the family unit. During the grieving process, this is what we all do. Although, because there's no conclusion to this, some people might say they are being a little premature.

Unless, of course, one of them knows something the rest of us don't. Could Josh, Sam, or Karen have anything to do with their disappearance? I think of jovial Josh and wonder - is he wearing this light-hearted expression to cover something up? Now I've met Sam, I decide she is an emotional wreck, but could Ellie's strange behaviour indicate that she knows something we don't and is manipulating Sam? And, Karen, in her red trouser suit, is as composed as ever, which makes me wonder - could she know something from the past about her parents that has reared it's ugly head. Through family honour, she would surely be the first to conceal an embarrassing event.

I know I've asked myself this before about these three siblings and dismissed the idea, but maybe there is something strange going on here? Karen interrupts my thoughts, and I turn to look at her.

Karen nods, 'Oh, yes, and the funeral down the country where the photograph was of a sat nav saying, "You've reached your final destination."'

We all laugh again as I think of how I talk to Doris and how much technology has, and still is, changing our way of life.

'Sorry, Faye,' Karen says. 'You'll think we are awful, talking about funny things that have happened, but in a way, it's our release valve.'

I nod in understanding. 'It's fine; I'm enjoying listening to all the aspects of funerals which, as I've said before, I know very little about,' I say. 'And I do remember, years ago, my friend's partner turning up at the wrong church and sitting through half the service before realising he was at the wrong funeral!'

They all laugh, and I can tell these black comic moments show the strong sibling bond while they cling to the hope and love that their parents will be found. They're still suffering from the impact of their parents' disappearance, which I liken to an unresolved trauma. However, these three will always have each other's backs, I reckon and I feel a pang of envy. Being an only child, it was the one thing I longed for growing up but never had.

Now they're all together, I decide it's the best time to tell them about Saltwell Park. I explain slowly what I discovered from the waitress in the Bewick tearoom but stress at least twice that she could be mistaken. 'I mean, she obviously remembers them, but she could have the date wrong, and it could have been months ago. And this won't be confirmed until the police can check the CCTV.'

Karen claps her hands together. 'I knew it!' She jumps up and begins to pace around the floor. 'I knew you'd come up with something, Faye.'

I sigh but take her slim hand as she passes by me. 'Thanks, Karen, but please, please, don't build your hopes up too high. I'd hate to see you all crash back down again.'

Josh grins. 'We understand, Faye,' he says. 'You know, I've been constantly asking myself the same questions since they went missing – how can this happen? I mean, with missing people and all the social media, internet, and mobiles – how do people stay off the grid and just disappear?'

'Well,' Karen says. 'We might just have caught them on the grid, Josh.'

Sam says, 'I saw Mam last night!'

We all stare at her, and my heart misses a beat. 'What?'

'It was about three o'clock in the morning. I saw the light in the hall go on as the bedroom door opened slightly. It didn't close again, and I saw Mam's shadow standing,' she whispers. 'And Mam said to me, "It'll be alright, Sam. I'm still here," and then she turned around and quietly left the room.'

My shoulders drop as Karen says, 'Oh, darling, it was just a dream.'

I can see the intense grief all over Sam's face because she doesn't know where her mam is, and I sigh heavily, feeling my throat tighten again. There's no closure for these siblings. I can tell, each one in their own way, is clinging to the hope that Violet and Lawrence will be found safe and well.

Sam shouts now and begins to sob loudly. 'It wasn't, Karen! I definitely saw her and heard her voice!'

Karen rushes to her side as Alfie slopes back to me, and I stand up to go, leaving them to their grief.

CHAPTER THIRTEEN
Sam Braithwaite

Sam is deep in thought sitting next to Ellie on the bus back into Newcastle from Birtley. It had never been easy visiting the family with Ellie, who usually based her moodiness on feeling left out. Today had been no different. Sam knew, however, that the deep-rooted reason was that she had never told the rest of the family about her sexuality.

Apart from getting upset at the end of the visit, Sam had liked meeting Faye, and, of course, Alfie was just a cuddly bundle of fun. It was true that she preferred talking to animals rather than human beings. They'd never hurt her before, and most animals wouldn't - as long as you didn't hurt them. She sighed, thinking, the same can't be said for people.

Sam had never felt wanted or understood, except by her mam, who smothered her. It would be awful if Mam didn't come home, but even worse if anything horrible happened to Karen – she couldn't cope with that. If Dad didn't come home, she knew, sadly, that she wouldn't bat an eyelid.

She shoved her hands into the pockets of her bomber jacket in an effort to stop picking the skin on her thumbs - one of her worst habits that she couldn't quit. Sam slyly glanced at Ellie from the corner of her eye. Ellie was staring out of the window, her lips twisted in a way that told Sam there would be an argument as soon as they got back to the flat.

Ellie tended to verbally punch first and ask questions later, which Sam knew was just her nature.
It was these actions that revealed her girlfriend's true character. When they first met, she had said, 'I'm only looking after myself nowadays and no one else.'

However, Sam watched Ellie show acts of kindness to friends and her siblings, proving that she wasn't selfish at all. Like Sam, she had a troubled childhood that impacted on her teens and then adulthood as a young woman. It was what had cemented them together from the beginning.

Sam had met Ellie two years ago at a craft fair in Jesmond, where she'd gone to look at a local artist's paintings. Ellie's stall was full of beautiful handmade greetings cards. There had been a certain twinkle when their eyes met, and Sam bought birthday cards for her mam and Karen later that year. It had been a ruse to keep Ellie talking to her, and Sam had seen how well thought of she was by other stallholders. They arranged to meet for coffee at the end of the fair. They talked for an hour that day, and Sam knew it wouldn't be the last time she saw Ellie.

Their first date was for a drink in Newcastle, and Sam had wound herself into a frenzy hours before the allotted time. Karen had told her, 'Look, Sam, just be yourself and tell her how you are and what you feel. Be upfront from the start, and if Ellie runs for the hills, then it's not meant to work out. But you'll never know unless you try!'

They'd sat in a pub full of students and goths, with loud music blasting. Sam had wrung her hands together under the table with bright lights in her eyes making her blink more rapidly – it was something she usually tried to avoid.

Remembering Karen's words, she had taken a deep breath and told Ellie, 'I've no confidence in myself other than in my artwork, where I can let myself go and know what I do is good – but still, I can't shout it from the rooftops.'

Ellie had taken her hand and squeezed it firmly. 'It's okay, I'm listening.'

Sam had continued. 'Since I was little, I've tended to think visually rather than in words, and I often draw sketches to explain how I feel.' She had paused to take another deep breath. 'I…I've always loved routine and collecting things – it feels like a comfort blanket to me. And, like now, I often feel overwhelmed in unfamiliar situations.'

Sam had sat back, slumping in the chair, exhausted from bearing her soul. She had wondered whether Karen had been right and Ellie would run for the hills. But she hadn't. Instead, Ellie had cupped Sam's face in her own trembling hands and kissed her long and hard. Sam hadn't gone home for three days, staying in Ellie's flat before moving in permanently within the month.

As the bus approached Low Fell, it was filling up with passengers, and Sam felt her knees twitch – being surrounded by people was something she hated. She practised her distraction techniques, letting her mind wander back to her childhood home on Long Bank.

She had never felt close to Dad. Watching American TV shows in her teens, she had envisioned close family units which were wholesome when the father came through the door from work and there was laughter, wisecracks, and hugs for everyone. It created a lovely close atmosphere where the whole family lived well together. And Sam had wanted that for her family, but it never happened.

Instead, her dad had been aloof with a total lack of cuddles from him, but she did have plenty of extra hugs from Mam and Karen. She knew this had been to make up for Dad's cold distance. Mam spoilt her, and even now, Sam still relied upon her for every thing. Josh reckoned Dad had been the same with him, but her brother teased her mercilessly from being little. This gave Sam a deep-rooted dislike of men that had never left her.

At the age of twelve, a psychiatrist had confirmed that her aversion to men stemmed from her dad's rebuke. Even the shrinks had been men, and another one had labelled her as bordering on autism, a term she hadn't understood. Her mam had been horrified and furious in equal measure at this label. Sam had heard her badgering Dad for money to get a second opinion, counselling, and further assessment. Begrudgingly, he had agreed.

Before leaving school, Sam had explained to another male shrink, I like to lose myself in artwork, and the thought of working in an office with other people terrifies me.

He had replied, In that case, you'll never be a useful member of society.

Once again, Mam had ranted and raved about this and wanted to make a complaint, but all it did was make Sam feel different to her siblings. She'd said, But, Mam, this means I'm getting more than Karen and Josh were given!

Mam had explained, No, they're older and get their wages from the business, which you don't, so it works out evenly. Also, you're the only member of the family with artistic talent, and you need to make the most of the gift you've been given.

Sam had told Ellie all about this dislike of men when they first met, and she understood. Ellie had gently probed about abuse - both verbal and sexual - but Sam had cried, 'Oooh, no! Dad is a doctor – he'd never do anything like that!'

Ellie had kindly explained how abusers and predators came in all forms and from all walks of life, no matter what occupations a man held. She had finished by saying, I think it sounds more like neglect by your father.

***

After changing buses in Newcastle, they arrived back into the flat, and Sam went straight into what they called their craft room. It was basically a large second bedroom, where Ellie had a small desk in the corner with her card-making materials, and in the opposite corner, Sam had her easel and art supplies.

Sam pulled off her bomber jacket and stared at the canvas on the easel, which she had started two days ago. It was a black and grey sketch of a tortured woman's face, which is how she saw her mam.

Sam could feel Ellie at her shoulder and knew she would start fuming about the visit to Karen's. She knew the main bone of discontent between them was that she couldn't tell the rest of her family she was gay.

Ellie had come out to her family years ago and wanted Sam to do the same. Sam knew it made Ellie feel trivial and unimportant in her life, which wasn't true - she was closer to Ellie than anyone she had ever been and told her this regularly.

  Picking up a paintbrush, she scored a black streak across the canvas and muttered, 'Please don't say anything today, Ellie. I'm trying to avoid more stress at all costs. With Mam and Dad missing, I'm near to tipping over the edge!'

115

CHAPTER FOURTEEN
The old cinema at Beamish Museum

As I crunch through a bowl of cereal, my phone rings, and I smile, taking the call from Penny. Swallowing down the mouthful of muesli, I tell her about Karen, Josh, and Sam, who I've met, without using their names for confidentiality purposes.

'Actually,' I say, 'the eldest daughter reminds me a little of you - with her lovely clothes and style - and how other people thinks she's closed-up and constrained.'

She laughs. 'As long as I'm like her and not the younger, neurotic sister!'

'I didn't say she was neurotic – just an emotional wreck,' I say. 'But she's young and missing her mam.'

I hear her pause and know she's being reflective about her past when she says, 'Well, as you know, I wouldn't have cried if my mum had gone missing.. In fact, she did - for weeks on end, on a drugged-up bender - when I was left to God and his good neighbour. But I would have cried back then if your mam had gone!'

Nobody but me knows, Penny's vulnerable side and the miserable, upsetting childhood she'd had. Even now, she has nightmares about it. I know her inner fear of not being loved - or being loved by the wrong relative. My mam had once said of her, 'Underneath the fun and gaiety lies a troubled soul.'

That was when my mam had taken her into our home like a waif and stray. After a hot bath, Mam fed her and made sure our spare bed was always clean and warm for her.

Penny cheers her voice and says, 'Well, as soon as you've found your missing parents, I'll come up to South Shields for a long weekend, and we can laze on the beach like we did last year.'

'Yeah,' I say. 'Lets do that, although you'll have to keep an eye on the forecast because it's changeable.'

***

I set off to Beamish Museum, following Doris on the sat nav. Driving down a road onto Station Lane, I follow a small green bus with "28" and "Beamish Museum" on the front. I nod in satisfaction, knowing I'm on the right track. I remember Karen saying they have a good bus service in Birtley, with buses running regularly from Durham City through to Newcastle Upon Tyne.

We pass up and over a bridge across the main railway line into Newcastle Central Station and then turn left into the countryside, passing through the villages of Ouston and Pelton. The pink and purple hues of heather on the hills are a sight to behold, and I'm loving the journey so far.

The village of Beamish has big, old, stone-built houses, with a few tastefully built new ones thrown into the mix. Alfie is looking out of the window, and I talk to him while driving. 'Oh look, Alfie, that small street sign reads "Peggy's Wicket!"' I giggle. 'What a funny name.'

There's a big pub and restaurant, Shepherd and Shepherdess, on the corner, and then I follow the bus through huge red colliery gates with the sign: *Beamish Museum, The Living Museum Of The North.*

I cry out, 'We're here!'

Parking up, we walk down a gentle ramp in front of a two-storey, long, white building with windows and pink doors. There are two big archways in the centre, with a clock above, and the sign reads *Main Entrance.*

A few people are milling around, but there's no queue, and we enter the building to be greeted by staff in traditional 40s costumes, serving people tickets. I notice it's dog-friendly but keep Alfie on his short lead.

Buying my ticket, I'm told it lasts for a year, so I can return as often as I like, and I'm given a pretty visitor map. Unfortunately, the trams are not running today as they're repairing tracks on the line. I smile, thinking of our LNER service - there's no change there, then from the 1950s.

I'm directed out through the room with history boards informing visitors how the first collections were put into the museum in 1970, when our old Queen Mother opened the museum. Following other people down to the bus stops, I look at my map and notice the museum is set out in a circular route, where we can hop on and hop off the buses at the six stops. Or, of course, we can walk the route, but I decide to take the bus.

Karen had said her parents had been here a few weeks before they disappeared, and my main purpose for the visit is to talk to staff in different areas and show the photograph of Violet and Lawrence to see if they can remember them.

I decide to head to the old cinema first, in the 1950s town, which, according to the map, is the second stop.

The red bus with open doorway and circular steps up to the top deck makes me smile, with an old advertisement on the side for *Watson's Toffees.* Inside, a plaque states it's from the Sunderland depot, 1947.

I'm thrilled when the conductor, in his uniform, shouts, 'Hold tight, please!' and, with a ding-dong jingly bell we set off.

Alfie is up on my knee, thoroughly enjoying the adventure. I stroke his ears, knowing many dogs don't like buses and train journeys, but this has never affected Alfie. In fact, nothing much does. Guy Fawkes Night with its loud fireworks and bangers, passes him by, where other dogs quiver and hide in fright.

We pass the 1820s Pockerley Old Hall landscape, then reach the 1950s town and we hop off the bus onto the front street. It's a short, cobbled-stone street with the cinema in the centre and another road heading up to a small park and bandstand.

There are a few houses to look inside, one in particular owned and lived in by a music teacher and singer. It's delightful, showing the old piano and furniture in a front parlour. A staff member, in a white cook's apron and a white frilly mop cap, is in the kitchen baking bread in front of a roaring fire. She reminds me of the cook from *Downton Abbey* TV show. With hands covered in flour, she bends forward to look at my photograph but shakes her head, not recognising the couple.

Across from this house is the big *Co-operative Society Department Store*, and I love looking at all the timeworn kitchenware and produce. There's an old wooden cabinet with glass shelves holding ancient pill and medicine bottles, with a sign on top reading *Druggists' Sundries.* As a doctor, I bet Lawrence would have enjoyed seeing this blast from the past, but I receive another shake of the head from the man behind the counter when I show him my photograph.

The tramway and Omnibus waiting room is empty, and I bypass the Masonic Hall and Barclays Bank buildings. Next to this is a red, brightly painted handcart full of Suffragette memorabilia. I smile and whisper, 'Go, Ladies, Go.'

Reaching the bottom of the street, I stop at a 1950s café with wooden booths, milkshakes, frothy coffee, and an old jukebox playing Elvis songs. I hum along while showing the lady behind the counter the photograph, but again, she shakes her head.

We stop outside *Middleton's Fish and Chip Shop,* and the smell makes my stomach rumble. Alfie cocks his head up at me, and I know he's hungry too. Standing in a short queue, I notice people carrying out their fish and chips in cone-shaped newspaper wrappings. What a great marketing ploy, I think. I buy Alfie a sausage and myself a small battered fish, feeling rather proud of myself for resisting the chips - but I soak my fish with salt and vinegar.

Finding a bench outside, Alfie wolfs down his sausage while I enjoy my fish, reading articles from the *Darlington Despatch,* which must have been an old newspaper company. Why did we stop using newspapers and replacing them with plastic containers? However, when the vinegar drips out of the bottom of the cone and onto my jeans, I curse and know the reason why.

Fed and watered, we cross the cobbled street to the cinema. I know Lawrence had wanted to see this, and how it was re-built.

The cinema has been reconstructed in light red brick with bright green boarding and lights underneath the huge sign, *GRAND*.

I take photographs and learn inside how the cinema depicts the golden age of film, with framed photographs on the walls of Marilyn Monroe, Frank Sinatra, and Doris Day, to name but a few.

Apparently, the original Grand cinema first opened in 1913 and is from Ryhope in Sunderland. Instantly, I think of Olivia and wonder if they'd like to visit the museum during the school holidays.

I read how it has been recreated and brought to life, screening films, period newsreels and adverts. The Grand was hugely popular in its heyday in the 1950s, often selling out the seats. It originally closed in the 1960s and later became a bingo hall, but it was then donated to the museum by Angela and Gary Hepple. In 2020, The Grand was dismantled, and any re-usable parts brought to Beamish to be incorporated into the cinema.

There's no one around in the foyer at the brightly painted, old-fashioned ticket booth, but I take photographs, marvelling at the art décor fixtures and fittings, the red and gold carpeting, and the white shell-shaped wall lights.

I head inside the auditorium and gasp in awe at the two huge stained-glass windows positioned on either side of the cinema screen. These had been carefully removed from Sunderland and incorporated into the rebuild. The auditorium includes a stage, screen, brown pit benches, and the more expensive red upholstered seats with matching red carpeting throughout.

Taking a seat on the third row, I decide to watch the short film.

I hear a lady behind me say, 'Have you noticed the two seats joined together for courting couples?'

Her husband laughs. 'We're too old to sit in them now, pet.'

I muse, yeah, but me and John aren't, and I smile at the old word, courting. Is that what John and I are? I wonder. And will we still be together in our older age like the couple behind me?

The screen appears, and I watch old adverts with the *British Pathe* logo in the corner. Ex-Lax for constipation, Walter Wilson's, Lyon's ice cream, OXO cubes, and then an advert about building new houses every month. I sigh, wondering how our construction companies nowadays can't follow their lead from the 50s.

A short sci-fi film begins about flying sauces in black and white, and then at the end, it tells us all, 'To mind how we go.'

So friendly and pleasant, I think, now leaving the auditorium, knowing that Lawrence would have loved this experience, especially the reconstruction aspects.

When I return to the foyer, I see a member of staff by the ticket booth wearing a brown trilby and dressed is a striped waistcoat and wool jacket. He's very tall and thin and is chatting to some visitors.

I wait patiently and then approach him with my photograph of Viole and Lawrence. We get off to a good start when he pets Alfie, and a big grin shows off his sparkly eyes.

I show him the photo and say, 'I know it's a long shot because you must see hundreds of people, but do you remember this couple who were here about three weeks ago?'

He looks down at the photo for a few seconds and then nods. 'Oh, yes, I do remember them – well, at least the man, because he was snappy and shouting at his wife, who looked like a shy, quiet, mouse-like lady.'

I sigh, knowing this is Lawrence's abrupt manner, which other people have already told me about. It's obvious that strangers do not take kindly to Lawrence, especially if they don't know he's a doctor. However, I think, this shouldn't make any difference – it should be common curtesy from one person to another. I smile. 'Ah, right, I don't suppose you can remember anything he said?'

The man rubs his clean-shaven chin. 'Well, I remember him shouting, "I've told you that three times in the last hour! And I'm not telling you again - you need a hearing aid!" I felt sorry for her as she seemed to shrink inside herself whilst clinging onto his arm. He looked like a bully, which made my heckles rise.'

My heart starts to beat faster, and I rush at my words. 'H...Hey, that's great. Can you remember when that was?'

He scratches his mop of black curly hair. 'Em, not really – I think it could have been around Easter time,' he says. 'But I couldn't say for sure.'

My hands go limp, and I push the photo back into my bag. 'Not to worry,' I say, 'but thanks anyway.'

Outside, we wander back around to the bus stop, and I sit on the bench with Alfie looking up at me. I whisper, 'Let's go to the 1940s farm, and you can have a run on your long lead.'

My insides feel deflated because, for a few moments, I'd thought I was onto to something with the usher at the cinema. However, I shrug. At least I know they were her, but when this was, is a different matter. And, as the bus trundles up to the stop, I think, and where they are now is anybody's guess.

On the bus, I marvel at how many young people there are visiting the museum. I'd figured that a museum set from the 1800s to the 1950s would hold the most attraction for the elderly, but not so - it's obviously being enjoyed by all ages and families. Following a stretch of our legs at the farm areas, we walk back to the car park.

***

Driving back to Birtley, I sigh at another dead end to the mysterious disappearance of Violet and Lawrence. Although, the cinema usher did remember them being there, I don't have a definite date like I did in Saltwell Park. While pulling into the car park at the Angel Hotel, I wonder if the museum has CCTV?

CHAPTER FIFTEEN
Violet Braithwaite

Out of her three children, Violet worried most about her youngest, Sam. She looked around at the few possessions she'd brought with her - a meagre amount to reflect her life and achievements.

'Don't bring loads, ' her husband had warned. And, as usual, she did what he bid.

Last month, she had seen a medical report on his desk while he was at the pool swimming. It read: 'The conclusion is that this patient has the beginnings of dementia.'

Laurie had highlighted this sentence, but there was no name on the report. She had supposed it could have been about one of his old patients. However, she knew he was up to something. You don't live with someone for over forty years without knowing when they are behaving strangely.

He kept forgetting things and would slap his forehead, exclaiming, 'Names! Names!'

He seemed to be losing his patience with her, becoming more irritable than ever. In the past, he had behaved like this when his plans weren't working out the way he wanted. Afterwards, he would apologise and buy her theatre tickets or treat her to a restaurant meal. And, of course, she had always forgiven his manner and behaviour for the sake of the children growing up and their treasured family life. But now, it was happening all of the time.

Violet looked around the unfamiliar small bedroom while perched on the end of the bed. She picked up the small silver photograph frame she had always loved.

It held a smaller version of the large framed family portrait that hung on the wall at Long Bank.

She ran her thumb down the side of her husband's face in the photograph, remembering how much she had loved him over the years. She was the only person who called him Laurie and had done from the first day they met.

In front of him, with her shoulders pulled back, stood proud, confident Karen, who was the spitting image of her dad. Next to her, with a big grin on his sweet face, was Josh, her middle child - sensitive, caring, and funny. Violet herself stood at the back with her arms wrapped around young Sam, who scowled in front of her – she had always hated having her photo taken.

Violet stared at her own image, wearing a blue summer dress and a self-satisfied expression on her face. She had been, and still was, proud of her family and the funeral business logo on the board behind them all.

She had met Laurie when he finished his internship at the Queen Elizabeth Hospital in Gateshead and had taken a GP role at a surgery in in Birtley. He hadn't been a particularly good-looking man, but had bright blue eyes that twinkled when he said, 'Because I'm an only child, I'd love to have a big family - maybe two or three children!'

Violet had swooned and agreed with him. In later years, she would use the modern day expression that he had 'ticked all her boxes'. She had thrown herself into making the funeral business a success and raising their family.

But now, she frowned. Laurie was prepared to just disappear without a word to the family. .

The day before they left, he'd said, 'We're going on a small trip, and I don't want you to say a word to anyone about it - not even the kids. It's got to be top secret!'

However, she had been unable to do this. She had taken a small writing pad and pink envelope from the bureau at home. Whatever Laurie's plans entailed, she didn't know - he kept telling her it was all a 'big surprise.' But Violet suspected it had connotations of not being very pleasant at all.

Swallowing a lump in her throat, she wrote:

'My darlings, I know you'll be shocked to read this letter but I didn't want to leave without you all knowing how much I love you - my babies. You have been the most important thing in my life, and I will take you all with me in my heart. In case I don't see you all again, please stick together. The three of you can give each other support and love, whatever comes in your future lives. Love you always, Mam.'

Violet had hesitated over how to address the envelope but then remembered a sentence from a book she had read. Wiping away a tear from her cheek at the thought of not seeing her children again, she wrote, 'To be read in the event of my death.'

The sound of Laurie taking off his boots at the back door had made her hurriedly tuck the letter inside one of her library books.

Now, she laid back on the bed, her head sinking into soft, squashy pillows.

She smiled. deciding to think of nicer memories. She would always remember meeting Malcolm as her last happy summer.

She'd been lonely when Laurie was constantly working at the surgery. And that was when she'd had a fling with Malcolm Jenkins, a man from Cambridge who had come to bury his father. He'd only been in town for a month, to empty his father's home and sort out his affairs with a solicitor in Chester-Le-Street. The property was a large terraced house on Orchard Terrace, with an allotment across the back lane.

Violet grinned now, remembering that first day working alongside him in the allotment. While he was filling his time between solicitor, estate agent, and bank appointments, she had been watching him. They'd dug up potatoes, onions, and selected the best tomatoes. Violet spent her time looking at him with her heart racing and a dry mouth as they talked.

The following day, she'd chosen her most provocative outfit and had watched his eyes roam over her body. She knew he felt the same. Within hours, they had made love in the large garden shed, over bags of compost. It had been wonderful - he was gorgeous, sexy, and everything that Laurie wasn't.

'Come back to Cambridge with me,' he had begged.

She had refused knowing she couldn't leave her family or the business. From the first day with Malcolm, she'd known she would never see him again, which had made it all the more exciting and eased her conscience. Her mantra had always been never to mix business with pleasure, especially when people were vulnerable and grieving. But Malcolm had been the opposite of vulnerable – he was confident, funny, with lovely manners, and very comfortable in his own skin which had made him irresistible.

Afterwards, when Malcolm was back in Cambridge, Violet missed a period. She seduced Laurie to cover her tracks. Briefly, she considered an abortion but shuddered - she couldn't go through with it. And, of course, back then, it wasn't as straightforward as it is now.

However, when Sam was born, Violet rued the day she'd had these thoughts because Sam was a beautiful baby. She had her struggles from being a little girl, but Violet believed it was simply because everyone, including herself, compared her to Karen, her eldest. Which hadn't been fair.

Of course, Sam wasn't Laurie's child, though he didn't know this. That was why her little girl bore no resemblance to any other family members. For all of Sam's life, Violet had thought she'd got away with her indiscretion. But two months ago, a letter had arrived from Cambridge. With trembling hands, she had opened the envelope.

'I'd like to know for certain whether your youngest girl, Samantha, is in fact my daughter.'

Panic had surged through Violet until her legs shook. She'd sat forward in a chair, taking deep breaths until her heart rate slowed.

Apparently, Malcolm had found Sam on Facebook and noticed the resemblance to him and his family. It had been a friendly letter, not accusing her but saying how he'd married again. Sam was exactly like his own daughter, Anne.

Violet had thought of her neighbours, friends, and especially Sam finding out about her transgression. Her face burned with shame. She'd also known the deceit to Laurie would be unbearable. She knew something awful was going to happen. But Laurie couldn't have seen the letter – she had burnt it straight away.

Sighing heavily, she thought, we might as well both be dead – Laurie would make her life a misery.

As her eyelids drooped and sleep came upon her in this unfamiliar bed, she wondered how different her life might have been if she had gone to Cambridge and left Laurie.

CHAPTER SIXTEEN
A much needed catch-up

I'm back in my hotel room with Alfie asleep on the floor in front of the window. He's had a good run around the grounds at Beamish, and my legs are tired too. The hotel have been great, accepting my stay on an ad-hoc basis depending on how long I'm going to remain in Birtley. It's five days now, and I'm still enjoying the case, but I wish I could find out more.

Plus, of course, I'm missing John more than I thought possible. Even though I don't spend many night times in my own flat, I'm used to being there during the day.

A tinkle from my mobile alerts me to a message from Olivia. Whether it's because I've been surrounded by a family for days, I suddenly have the urge to hear my daughter's voice, so I ring Olivia instead of texting. She sounds just as happy to hear my voice as I am to hear hers.

She tells me about what she calls her mundane life on the school run and housekeeping this week. We discuss washing curtains, and I'm loving every moment. Olivia tells me that the girls have asked where I am this week and how she explained that I'm helping out a family whose parents are missing. They thought it was very careless of a family to lose their mam and dad and had collapsed into fits of giggles.

We laugh together now, and I love her soft, throaty laugh. I imagine her gentle face with long blonde hair tied back in a ponytail and her blue, sparkly eyes. She's always been the double of her dad, and thankfully, I've often told her that she hasn't inherited any of my features. We end the call, and I sigh, with longing to see them all soon. When I'm not working, I often pop over to Sunderland to spend time with them once a week, and I promise to do so as soon as I wrap this case up.

I think of all my years with Allan and how Olivia was born into so much love and adoration from us both. I'd strived to give her the best childhood ever, and she had been our main focus right up until she married. Well, until now, really, because she still is.

I remember my daily routine and love of writing - working with editors, cover designers, the endless book signings and talks. It had been non-stop. As soon as my first novel was successful, they wanted me to write another, and I'd jumped onto the merry-go-round of publishing high-quality crime novels. As our daughter grew older, I scheduled my writing in between Olivia's school activities. I'd drop her off and write straight through until it was time to collect her again and prepare tea. The older she got, the more activities progressed into athletics, dance classes, and sleep overs. I would often snatch two hours between these sessions, writing here and there to meet deadlines, chapter after chapter, until I could finally type the blessed words: "The End."

I sigh now wondering how I ever managed to fit all of that into my life and feel my stomach rumble. I've brought a sandwich back from Beamish Museum and tuck into it as Alfie wakes and eats his dinner. As I eat, I can't help wondering how Olivia would feel if I disappeared and was missing. Would she react like Karen? And although she looks like her dad, she has a bright, inquisitive mind, and I've often called her my kindred spirit. Therefore, I know she'd be organising the search and hounding the police until she was satisfied with their enquiries. And, of course, I know she would be devasted at my absence.

My thoughts drift back over the day at the museum. I'd really enjoyed the outing and still feel soaked in the history of the place and the region. It's a great museum, obviously very clean and well cared for by helpful staff. I can see they're proud of the museum and the effort they make each day for visitors to appreciate the history of our region. It was also easy to navigate using the map. Let's face it, I think - if I can use the map and not get lost, anyone can.

I'd bypassed Pockerly Old Hall from the 1820s, which I would still love to see, and the pit village and colliery, although they do have an amazing old coal waggon at the entrance. Still, mining is part of the North's history, and I know John would love to see it too.

I have a lightbulb moment and decide to take John to the museum as a lovely birthday surprise in September. Hopefully, the weather will still be good, and in my mind, I start to plan the weekend. We could stay somewhere more rural, in a countryside cottage, which would be romantic. Or - I pause, thinking of the courting couple seats in the cinema - I'll make it romantic.

Shaking myself back to the case, I think of meeting the three siblings together at Karen's house and my thoughts about them. As I've met Josh, I reach over for his index card and write: 'A jovial man with a carefree attitude, but is this covering up something? Is he upset when alone and just putting on a brave face in front of his sisters?'

My thoughts turn to Sam now. And on her Index card, I write: 'An emotional wreck with a weird partner, Ellie, who certainly seems to rule the roost. Are they covering up something to do with Lawrence?'

I take Karen's card, which I'd previously written on, and add under her possible co-codamol addiction: 'Could she know something from the past about her parents that has reared its ugly head. I'm sure, through family honour, she would be the first to hide an embarrassing event.

Drinking my coffee, I sigh. I've asked myself this before of these three siblings and dismissed the idea, but maybe there is something strange going on here. Could Josh, Sam, or Karen be involved in anyway with their parents' disappearance?

This is the intriguing side to mysteries that I love. It keeps me guessing about people and, how they fit together in their backstories leading up to an event. I shrug. And an elderly missing couple is definitely an event - or happening - we don't see everyday.

I know Karen has rung the policewoman leading the case, and I've written down her name: Mira Patel. This has a nice ring to it, I think, and I dial the number for Gateshead Police Station, where she works. I leave a message for her to contact me and am surprised when, fifteen minutes later, she rings back.

I introduce myself, and at first, I hear a slight snort in her voice when I use the title 'amateur sleuth'. However, I persevere. 'So, I decided to go to their favourite places, and I spoke to the waitress in Bewick Tearooms, who told me that she remembered them.'

'Oh, right,' she says. 'So you're Faye, the one Karen has been telling me about.'

Alongside a slight Asian accent, I now hear a lift of approval in her voice. 'Yeah,' I say. 'It's me, and I wondered if you'd had the chance to look at the CCTV yet?'

'I have to say, that was a great idea, thanks,' she says. 'So, where else have you been looking for them?'

I tell her about Birtley High Street, the library, Morrisons, and the swimming pool. We chat easier now, and I can almost see her shoulders drop as she realises I'm not a threat to their investigation.

Sleuthing is often a strange position, although last year in South Shields, it seemed easier because I'd fallen for the police inspector in charge of the investigation at the guest house. However, at first, before John and I got to know each other,. he had been reticent too. But once I told him details about the other holiday makers and he realised I had a suspicious mind, he soon valued these facts. What I'd discovered had all helped to build up the case and find the culprit.

Mira continues. 'So, the CCTV actually caught Violet in a grey mack and Lawrence wearing a brown jacket, getting in and out of their car at 12 5noon and returning at 3 p.m. It is dated, so we definitely know they were alive and well five days after they disappeared. But where they are now is a different story, isn't it?'

Holding the mobile at my ear, I jump up and dance around the room with delight.

I cry. 'Finally, Thank God we have something concrete!'

Alfie jumps up with me, bears his teeth, and I'm sure he is laughing too. Of course, I'm thrilled for Karen, Josh and Sam, but I'm also delighted that all my efforts have proved fruitful and might just help in some way to find them.

Plenty of people say that, as an amateur sleuth, I've nothing to lose and am well paid. In some respects, this is true, but apart from solving the mystery, I want to give good value for my fees.

I can almost here Mira smile as she asks, 'And have you any other ideas up your sleeve, Faye?'

Now I grin from ear to ear because she is taking me seriously and talking as a fellow professional – something John has always done.

I nod. 'Well, actually, I've been up to Beamish Museum today because that's another place they loved to visit, and Lawrence was especially interested in their newly rebuilt cinema.'

'Oh, right,' Mira says. 'And did you find out anything more?'

I shrug. 'Well, the usher at the cinema recognised them from their photograph but can't remember when it was. So, I wondered if Beamish Museum have CCTV as well?'

'That's something I can find out, and if so, I'll get recordings for the last two weeks. Although we keep checking both their mobiles, since the Monday when they were still at home, there has been no activity. So, Faye, keep up the good work, and we'll speak soon.'

This makes me feel taller and stronger, and I take in a deep, satisfied breath. I know Karen appreciates the work I've done so far, and of course, John is full of praise, but to have this recognition form a stranger and - a police detective - pleases me no end.

We agree to keep in touch, and I promise to let her know if I come up with any other information. We exchange mobile numbers, and I celebrate my success by eating the two biscuits on the tea tray provided by the hotel staff.

I think of the lovely meals I've had in the hotel and at Alioli and cringe at the weight I'll have put on this week. Reasoning with myself, I decide that this case was an impromptu trip that I couldn't have foreseen and determine to eat salads for however much longer I'm here. Yeah, right, I think, knowing how weak my willpower can be at times.

Usually, I walk Alfie twice a day around the park, and I bend over to whisper to him, 'I think we'll be walking three times a day when we get home, matey.'

He looks up at me and thumps his tail. I know if I don't get a grip, I'll be returning to John with extra pounds hanging upon me, although he always says, 'Don't change a thing about yourself; I love you the way you are!'

I've never had much time for family cooking when I had been writing, but now there's just John and me to feed, I've thrown myself into trying new recipes. He seems to enjoy the new dishes, even the few that have turned out as a disastrous messes. On these occasions, I know he appreciates the effort I've made - whereas Allan would have binned my attempt and ordered a takeaway. And that, I smile is the difference.

With my mind back on the case, I send Karen a text. 'Hi, Karen. Great news! Mira tells me that they have got the CCTV, and the recording shows your mam and dad definitely in the park five days after they disappeared. They are getting out of their car at 12 noon and leaving at 3 p.m. Your mam is wearing her grey mack, and your dad a brown jacket. Speak later.'

My next call is to John, who is full of admiration for my achievements. I feel a mix of pleasure at hearing his kind words and pangs of longing to see him too. I think this is the longest we've been apart since we got together in South Shields last year, and I now realise how much I love him.

He makes me feel special, and making love to each other is a delight - so much so that my life would be bereft without our intimacy. I can't ever remember thinking this when I was with Allan, so the difference is stark and has given me a huge insight into what a couple should feel for each other.

CHAPTER SEVENTEEN
Karen Braithwaite

With her latest health routine in mind, Karen left her car at home and walked up to Long Bank to look for her mam's library books. She had found it hard to concentrate on paperwork and data sheets at the funeral business, so gave up and decided to do something more constructive.

It was great news that the police had checked CCTV at Saltwell Park and found them on camera. When reading the message, her knees had gone weak as hope surged through her - knowing that they were still alive and well on the Friday after they left. She murmured, Please, God, let them still be all right.

If only they knew that Mam and Dad were still alive and well somewhere, the situation wouldn't seem so bad. Her stomach churned, but she put a spring in her step, relieved that she hadn't succumbed to her medication for thirty-six hours now. However, as she crossed the road, she sighed - counting hours in her habit still wasn't something to be proud of.

Out of the three of them left behind, Karen was most worried about young Sam, who was distraught over their parents' disappearance. And, she wasn't sure how to handle her sister.

Managing Sam was something Mam had always done. As she walked up the bank, she wondered what Mam would do if she was here. Instantly, she heard her voice in her mind: 'At least Sam is letting out her emotions in tears, but in a way, Josh is more of a worry because he's bottling everything up and hiding behind his comic façade.'

Karen knew this was true. And, as usual, she tried to keep herself in check by following a strict routine – anything to avoid outright hysteria.

***

It was quiet around the outside of her parents' house as she slid her key in their door. She walked into the lounge, looking around the room for library books, and figured they must be upstairs on Mam's bedside cabinet.

She glanced at Dad's fireside chair and gulped down a huge ball of misery in her throat. Then, murmuring into the silence, she whispered, 'Oh, Dad, where are you? And why would you do this to us?'

Wearily, she climbed the stairs and found two books next to Mam's side of the bed. She paused, trying to remember Faye's conversation. Had she said there were two books out on loan from the library or three? She shrugged, knowing the library would have a record. If there was three, perhaps Mam had taken the third book with her - wherever the hell they were.

Karen shivered. It wasn't cold in the house as the sun was shining, but it felt eerie and strange to keep coming inside when they were absent. Although, it was their family home, the house she had grown up in, somehow, it didn't feel like home at all. As she locked the front door behind her, she grimaced. Would Mam and Dad ever return to this house again?

***

A young girl was at the counter in the library and Karen explained the situation. With huge, gawky eyes, the girl leaned towards her, full of sympathy.

In a way, she reminded Karen of Sam, and she felt tears weren't far away. She swallowed hard and handed over the books.

The girl took the books and checked on her computer. 'Yes, there is a third book by Harlan Coben. It's his latest novel, I think. But don't worry - I can extend the loan for another three weeks,' she said. 'Then your mam can return it when she comes back.'

It was on the tip of Karen's tongue to say she didn't know when that would be. Suddenly, as the girl picked up the top book, an envelope fluttered onto the counter and she handed it to Karen.

The pink envelope was in her mam's handwriting. The words on the front sent a chill down her spine. 'To be read in the event of my death.'

Karen gasped and felt her heart begin to pound. Quickly, she pushed the envelope into her handbag before the girl could read the writing on the front. Desperate to get home, she hurried back outside wishing she had brought the car. Instead, she strode out in her new trainers up the road.

***

Back in her kitchen, she twirled the envelope over and over in her fingers. Her mind was in turmoil. She wasn't sure what to do – an unfamiliar feeling for her. Should she open it now? As far as they knew, Mam wasn't dead. And this was a private letter, not addressed to her. Yet, it might give them a clue about where they were. Maybe she should let Faye know and allow her to open it? Would there be fingerprints on the envelope and letter?

In an effort to think rationally, she pulled on her Marigold gloves and ripped the envelope open.

With shaking hands, she read the note twice as she stirred co-codamol into a glass of water.

'My darlings, I know you'll be shocked to read this letter but I didn't want to leave without you all knowing how much I love you - my babies. You have been the most important thing in my life, and I will take you all with me in my heart. In case I don't see you all again, please stick together. The three of you can give each other support and love, whatever comes in your future lives. Love you always, Mam.'

Tears streamed down Karen's face as her throat tightened painfully. She gulped hard and tore a piece of kitchen roll from the holder to dry her face.

What did this mean? The CCTV showed they were still alive last Friday. So, was this letter written after that day? But how? It was in her library book at home. Was Mam dead now? And was Dad dead, too?

If they were both still alive, why would Mam write a letter to be read after her death – unless, of course, she knew she was going to die? Were they in the hands of a madman, someone who had threatened to kill them while they were still at home?

Mam had obviously felt endangered. And in her own way, she had been defenceless. So where was Dad in all of this? Why hadn't he written a letter? Didn't he have something to say to them all? Especially to her, Karen thought with fresh tears spilling down her face.

She rubbed the base of her neck and shook her head. She couldn't figure this out and needed help. Faye's brain would be able to process it better - she wasn't emotionally involved in the same way.

And, Faye wasn't upset about their parents' and would think more clearly than she could.

Karen rammed the letter into her handbag and grabbed her keys. She needed to see Faye at the hotel. This could change everything. What had been a case of simply missing parents might now be something more sinister - possibly even dangerous.

Her mobile rang. She grabbed it, thinking it could be Lucca.

She had already decided not to tell him that his grandparents were missing until there was more definite news. She didn't want him worrying while he was away in York. Karen knew he would be devastated – especially about his grandfather. Like her, they were very close.

But it wasn't Lucca's name on the screen. It was Josh's.

She dabbed at her eyes with a tea towel and took three deep breaths in succession to steady herself. Shakily, she answered, 'Hello, there...'

Josh almost bellowed down the line. 'Karen! Karen! A postcard has arrived to the funeral parlour from Mam and Dad!'

'What!' She shouted, snapping into action.

'Look, ring Faye and tell her to come to yours ASAP!'

With her brain back in gear, she rang Sam. 'Get in a taxi straight away - I'll pay the driver when you get to Josh's house.'

CHAPTER EIGHTEEN
A postcard arrives

A text arrives on my mobile from Josh, asking me to come to the funeral business as soon as possible as something has happened. My mind is in a whirl as I pull on a clean yellow top and skirt. Shoving my feet into my sandals, I say to Alfie, 'Come on, Alfie, we're needed!'

He jumps up, and while I grab my handbag, he sits patiently by the door.

Jumping into my car, I don't need Doris because, after a few days in Birtley, I know the roads well enough by now. It's rush-hour traffic at the Angel of the North roundabout and I tap my hands on the steering wheel, muttering, 'Oh, come on, come on, let's go!'

The traffic moves, and I crawl down Durham Road at the assigned twenty miles an hour until turning onto the funeral parlour driveway. A taxi pulls up behind my car, and I see Sam climb out while Karen stands next to her, paying the driver. I unclip Alfie, and Sam greets me before taking Alfie's lead as he leaps out of the back of the car. He's used to her now and enjoys her fussing.

I greet Karen and notice it's the first time I've seen her dressed casually, although the jeans look designer, and she's wearing brand-new trainers, which wouldn't have been cheap either.

All of us hurry through the doors where Josh is waiting.

He says, 'Alice has prepared a tray of tea for us before seeing to the girls.'

He begins to pour out the tea into white mugs with their family logo on the side, then places a bowl of water on the floor for Alfie. I thank him.

I turn to Sam who has slumped down onto one of the sofas opposite Karen, and ask, 'Is Ellie not with you today?'

Sam shakes her head. 'No, she's doing a craft fair with her cards in Gosforth.'

I nod and settle onto the two-seater sofa next to Josh, who suddenly jumps up, almost jiggling from one foot to another with a little boy wonder look on his face. In a hoodie and jeans, he looks much younger than when wearing his business suit. I smile at him, knowing he is excited to be sharing his news.

With his hands behind his back, he cries, 'A card has arrived in the post, and it's in Dad's handwriting!'

As if he's a magician pulling a rabbit out of a hat, he whips the card from behind his back and holds it up high for us all to see. The photograph on the front is of The Angel of the North, which seems apt, I reckon, as it gives no clue as to where they are now.

Josh turns the card over and reads aloud: 'We love you all very much – sorry to leave like this. Mam & Dad.'

'Can I see?' I ask, holding out my hand. I think about fingerprints but know this will have been handled by many different staff in the post office before landing here, so it will be pointless. I turn over the postcard and muse, 'Well, it's got a Newcastle postmark on the second-class stamp.'

Wearing another creepy Goth T-shirt with a skeleton on the front, Sam looks as miserable and macabre as the image. She grunts. 'Hmmph, that's typical of Dad - not using first class because it's more expensive now!'

Karen drinks a mouthful of her tea. 'So, they must still be here somewhere – mustn't they?'

Josh nods and perches back onto the sofa next to me. 'Or they could be abroad and have asked someone to post it when they came home?'

Sam cries, 'Don't be stupid! When have they ever gone abroad? Scotland is the furthest they've ever been - to see the Edinburgh Tattoo - and they both came home with a cold because it never stopped raining for three days. Dad said, "Never again!"'

I know they are bickering between each other because that's what families do, and none of this will ever be mentioned or thought about again. As siblings, it's just who they are.

I sip my tea and add, 'Well, as the police often say, proof is everything in an enquiry. And they sometimes use the same three words: Love, Fear, and Money.'

Thinking of this, I wonder if Lawrence or Violet were having an affair or had been, and someone was looking for them. Was another partner involved? I smile and think, is it usual for older people to have affairs, divorce and re-marry? And does it usually involve drugs, alcohol, and fighting, like it does with younger couples? I haven't found any evidence to suggest this, but that's not to say it couldn't have happened, so I shouldn't rule it out.

I ask, 'Did they argue much lately, or was one of them acting out of character?'

'NO!' they all shout unanimously.

Josh drains his tea and clatters the mug noisily back onto the tray. I watch him take a deep breath and see his Adam's apple move up and down in his thin throat. He continues quietly, 'They were just their normal selves, Faye.'

Karen sits forward and looks directly at me. 'Dad treats Mam like a queen – he worships her. And Mam runs around him, catering to his every need. She mollycoddles him with love, like she does to all three of us.'

I nod, knowing we are back to the image of happy families once again. But is there something underlying this situation that they are all hiding? We haven't answered the motive of fear, and I wonder if their parents had an issue that scared them enough not to disclose it to their children. It's possible, I suppose, but I turn to Josh, who is speaking now.

'And I know their financial status as well as Karen does,' he says. 'Apart from the business, which is ours now, Dad recently told me there wasn't millions hidden away, but we'd all be comfortable. Therefore, it can't be anything to do with money!'

I thank him, and in my mind, I hear John's voice saying, 'Go back to the beginning and start again.'

I finish my tea and stand up. 'Look, lets just go through the last sightings again, just in case – we - or I - have missed something. No matter how trivial you think it is, just say it.'

Karen repeats her last text message to Violet aloud and shows the screen to me. 'This was on the Sunday night, and Mam replied, I'm busy at the moment – will ring you later.'

Karen shrugs, looking around at us all. 'But of course, she didn't.'

Josh says, 'And my family were with them on the Sunday morning for coffee and scones, which I've already said. They were both fine, and nothing was out of place.'

I start to pace around the small room which is what I often do when I'm thinking.

Sam takes her turn and says, 'Well, I spoke to Mam on the Monday.'

I ask, 'And what did you talk about?'

'Oh, just the usual,' she says, then screws up her top lip. Two big tears roll down her face. 'A...and I asked to borrow £50 and told her it was for photography stuff.'

She promptly bursts into sobs. 'B...but, it wasn't! It was to go out with Ellie and our friends to a nightclub!'

I can tell Sam isn't coping at all. Karen pats her arm in comfort.

Suddenly, Sam throws herself into Karen's arms and sobs. 'Ooooh, Mam, where are you?'

She begins to cry again, and Karen soothes her. 'It's okay to miss them, Sam. We all do.'

Gently, I ask, 'And did you get the money, Sam?'

She nods and dries her face with a tissue from Karen. 'Yeah, she transferred the money into my account – in fact, s...she gave me £100!'

I really feel for this family and know the mysterious disappearance is getting to me – it's driving me bonkers not knowing what's happened to their parents. And if this is chewing me up when I don't know Violet and Lawrence, God knows how they're feeling.

I sigh, remembering my dream last night and how I'd seen Lawrence's face hanging over my bed, staring at me, demanding to know where Violet was. His face was all twisted as he chewed on his moustache. It had been one of those panicky dreams when I woke up with a start, sweating and shivering. Alfie had crawled along the floor to me, whining and I'd found comfort in reassuring him that I was fine.

I take a deep breath and try to rationalise my thoughts and remain calm. I stand still in front of the vase of flowers on the windowsill and inhale the lovely fresh smell.

Josh cries, 'Oh, this is just an impossible situation – isn't it?'

To which we all agree. I can tell by their own personal grief that they want to talk about their parents all of the time, which is understandable. As Karen has said before, it keeps them close in a strange sort of way.

I say, 'Mira Patel needs to see this postcard straight away, Karen. Can you get her email address from the station and send a scanned copy to her?'

She nods miserably. 'Yeah, of course, I'll do it when I get back home on my printer.'

Josh sticks out what would have been his pet lip when he was little and gathers up the empty tea mugs. He mutters, 'No one is going to find them, and we'll have to live the rest of our lives not knowing where they are and what happened to them because they're simply gone!'

Sam blurts out, 'Well, Ellie reckons it was a terrible attack by a psychopath and they're already dead and buried in someone's garden.'

Josh tuts, and spittle from his mouth sprays slightly as he shouts at Sam. 'That's ridiculous! As I've told Alice – you're all watching too many police shows on TV!'

His sharpness towards his young sister makes me wince.

This is where I need to step in and try to bolster them up a little. 'Well, Josh, I'm trying my best, and I know we'll find them eventually. I'm not giving up!'

Karen says, 'If Dad had posted the card from Chopwell cottage weeks ago with a second-class stamp, it wouldn't have a Newcastle postmark.'

My ears prick up. 'What is Chopwell cottage?'

Josh explains. 'It's our cottage which we've had all our lives, about a 30-minute drive from Birtley. It's near Chopwell Woods, which is out west near Shotley Bridge and Rowlands Gill - have you heard of any of these places?'

I shrug my shoulders. 'Nope, I don't know the area, but my sat nav will get me there.'

They all start to talk about the cottage at once, and I look from one to another.

Karen says, 'It's miles from anywhere and was our safe haven where we all could relax and unwind. We loved it when we were younger. It belonged to Dad's father and he couldn't bear to sell it, although it's not much used nowadays.'

Josh says in a melancholy voice, 'It has a great river and woodland where we played for hours,' he chuckles. 'And inside the cottage, there's a row of wellington and hiking boots that have always stood at the back door, varying in sizes from biggest to smallest.'

Sam buts in. 'Don't get excited, Faye, because it was the first place we checked when they were missing. We went together in Karen's car, but there was no signs that they'd even been there for months.'

Kaen nods. 'Yes, there was milk in the fridge in lumps and cheese covered with mould. They hadn't been there for ages, but it was strange because Mam would never have left this stuff in the fridge. - she always cleared it out before driving back home.'

Josh shrugs. 'You're right, but I do think both of them were getting a little forgetful, which, of course, is probably just an old-age thing – isn't it?'

'Yeah, I suppose so,' Karen says and smiles. 'And it wasn't just us who loved the cottage because Dad often took Lucca up for the day to do things in the wood – he loved it.'

Josh tuts. 'Yes, but how come he refused to take my girls up there when Mam asked him?'

Karen teases, 'Ah, you've always been a mummy's boy!'

Josh jibes back, 'Well, you've always been a daddy's girl!'

Sam snarls, 'So where does that leave me?'

I tap my pen against the palm of my hand after writing down the address of the cottage and directions to Chopwell, knowing this will probably be my last enquiry because I'm running out of ideas. I get up, bid goodbye to them, and rescue Alfie from Sam's arms, and then leave the reception area.

CHAPTER NINETEEN
The pink envelope

As I head outside, Alfie hops onto the back seat of the car while I clip his harness into place. I turn around as Karen's voice calls me from behind. She gets into my car, and we drive up to her house.

The Holly's is busy, with people parking their cars – coming home from work, I presume. I pull up behind Karen's car. We don't get out but sit quietly together.

Karen says, 'I feel crap about this, but I couldn't bear to tell Josh and Sam what I found this afternoon. They're both so buoyed up after receiving the postcard.'

I raise an eyebrow. 'Okay, so tell me instead.'

From her handbag, she pulls out a clear plastic bag containing a small pink envelope. Her fingers tremble as she hands it to me. A single sheet of pink paper lies separately from the envelope but is still visible through the plastic. I tut to myself, knowing I should have had some disposable gloves in the car, but they're in my bigger bag at the hotel. I can tell this is going to be another key lead in the case, and feel a tingling sensation run through my fingers, itching to read what it says. I take a deep breath.

Karen nods slowly as I glance at her and see her eyes fill with tears. 'I put it into a clear plastic freezer bag and used my Marigolds because of fingerprints – just in case.'

I smile slightly but nod in appreciation of her forethought.

'It was tucked inside one of Mam's library books, which I found at their house next to her bed this afternoon.'

I read the sentence on the envelope and gasp out loud. A cold feeling creeps around my gut, and I shout, 'What the…'

'Just read the letter,' she murmurs.

Carefully, I hold up the plastic bag to the sunlight through the windscreen to see it more clearly.

I read the letter slowly, feeling my shoulders droop with each word, imagining the upset and hurt Karen must have felt when first reading it. 'Oh, Karen,' I mumble and reach to take her hand in mine.

But she sits upright, staring ahead out of the windscreen, both hands clasped tightly together on the clasp of her handbag. She is rigid, and I know her usual restraint is being tested to its limit.

I say, 'But your mam must have written this before they left Long Bank?'

'I know,' she says. 'She obviously knew something awful was going to happen. But what!'

She almost screams the last two words, and Alfie barks from the back seat. I reach behind and tickle his ear to soothe him. 'It's okay, boy.'

Karen nods. 'Sorry, but I can't figure it out. My mind is all over the place, and I thought you'd know what to do.'

I nod and speak slowly, keeping my voice calm to make sure she understands. 'Of course I know, Karen,' I say. 'You need to scan and email this, along with the postcard, to Mira with a note saying it's urgent.'

She nods miserably, and I can tell she understands. 'I'll ring the station and ask for her email address so I can send them straight away.'

More to herself, she mutters, 'Our Sam is in such a state - I couldn't show her. Or Josh, for that matter.

I think, in their own ways, they're clinging onto the edge of all this trauma, and it's probably best to wait until they've calmed down.'

She opens the car door to climb out and says, 'If that ever happens of course?'

CHAPTER TWENTY
Lawrence Braithwaite

Lawrence rubbed the red area on the side of his little toe. He'd brought the wrong shoes and left his more comfortable brown brogues in the bedroom at home. He tutted and kicked aside the black shoes that had tormented him for the last week staying up in Bamburgh overlooking the castle.

He'd taken Violet to their favourite places, Saltwell Park, and Beamish Museum before heading up the Northumberland coast. They'd stayed in a cosy little B&B and walked on the beach for miles.

Although, he mused, now they were here, there wasn't much more walking to do now. They were coming to the end.

It was strange how adamant he had been about sticking to his rules, making Violet do the same. He had thought she would be the one to weaken and contact the children, but it hadn't been her - it had been him.

Three days ago, he had succumbed and sent them a postcard. He had thought he could simply walk away with no goodbyes, but this had proved more difficult than he imagined. Now that the ending he had wanted and planned was in sight, he missed the children to such an extent that it troubled his conscience - especially, Karen and Lucca.

Was this what they called getting soft in old age? Violet had always been the weak one between them, but he had been stronger. Remembering the words he'd written on the postcard made him feel better. It meant they could leave this mortal coil without lingering bad feeling.

All was well, he thought, and sighed. There would be no more troubles of daily life to face.

He'd brought his two favourite books with him to read. He had probably read *Great Expectations* by Charle Dickens at least four or five times during his lifetime, but now he had read and enjoyed every word for the final time.

Lawrence looked across at Violet on the sofa, engrossed in a novel by her much-loved American crime writer. He knew she was lost in New York City, whereas he was in old Dickensian London with Pip and Miss Haversham.

These big differences between them had always existed since they first married, but seemed even more obvious now, during this last long period they had spent together.

Looking around the cottage lounge, which wasn't much different from when his father had bought and renovated it, he smiled at his childhood memories. The wooden walls, the measuring stick by the door marked with black felt-tip pen as his own children had grown taller and taller. The rattan sofa and chairs with big soft cushions that Violet had insisted on buying - although the original hard oak bench still stood in the corner adorned with a throw and cushions. His mother always complained about how uncomfortable it was, but he still enjoyed looking at it.

Karen and his grandson Lucca had often used the old bench, which pleased him enormously, although Josh and Sam were more often found sitting next to Violet on the new softer sofa.

He thought of Lucca now and grinned at the memories of their adventures out in the woods, making a new rope swing. Lawrence had taught him to play chess and recalled how the lad had been nearly as good as him and had beaten him at their last game. Lucca had a fun-loving nature growing up which had been so different to Josh.

Alice and Josh had fostered a boy called Alex, and Lawrence knew he should have made an effort to do something with him, but he hadn't - because Alex wasn't a Braithwaite. He wasn't his own flesh and blood. Josh, however, had accepted the boy as his own and taken him everywhere, which let Lawrence off the hook.

Perhaps it was true, as people often said, that being a grandfather was different. When you're older, you have more time to do things with children. Whereas, when Josh was young, Lawrence had been in the surgery treating patients twenty-four seven. But even as he thought it, he shrugged, knowing this was just an excuse.

Lawrence got up and wandered around the lounge, then into the small kitchen. Violet was still engrossed in her book, so he knew it was safe to check his drugs. The chloroform bottle was safely hidden in a paper bag in his holdall, on top of the wooden cupboard they used as a wardrobe. He knew she couldn't reach it.

However, the insulin vial was in the fridge, wrapped in an empty margarine tub with thick strapping around the outside, tucked away in the vegetable rack. The wrapping was still intact, so he knew Violet hadn't touched it. And, as she had done very little cooking since they arrived, he was confident it would be safe to use in the morning.

He thought of all the patients he'd treated and saved over the years but looking at his wife now, he knew there was nothing he could do to help her. He stood behind the sofa and gazed down at the top of Violet's head. He sighed heavily, knowing that his darling wife, whom he'd loved since the day they met, would soon go from the strong, clever matriarch of the family to a scared, pathetic housewife. And he couldn't bear to witness this decline. He had seen it too many times in his patients – it was such a cruel disease, and on the increase.

Lawrence had once heard a Macmillan nurse refer to dementia as *The Long Goodbye* - where, a person died little by little until their final demise. And that was the last thing he wanted for his wife. She deserved more than that – so much more.

However, if he didn't take her with him, she would find him dead, and that was grossly unfair. Violet didn't deserve that either – she would be hysterical, alone in the cottage. He sighed and thought he would face that decision nearer the time.

With the thought of tomorrow, he swallowed hard. During his career, he'd been with many people as they died, but of course, had never experienced the sensation of passing over himself.

Over the years, they'd attended Birtley Methodist Church for services, weddings, and christenings, but he wouldn't class himself as a religious man. He certainly knew that once the last breath left one's body, that was it. There was no coming back. He couldn't imagine his soul floating around in the atmosphere.

What would he feel? Pain? Or simply a loss of all sensations in his body as his muscles slackened and drowsiness overtook him. Maybe there would be a feeling of nothingness as his brain stopped working, starved of oxygen. He did hope he wouldn't wet himself - because it could be months before they were found.

His original plan had been to put an end to them both, but now the time was upon him, he chewed the end of his moustache. Was he truly capable of doing this to her? Ending her life as well as his own?

Before leaving home, he'd looked up the definition of self-sacrifice. It was *The giving up of one's own interests or wishes in order to help others or advance a cause.*

He thought of their deaths as self-sacrifice - to avoid the cruel fate of living with dementia. They had always gone everywhere together, and he couldn't bear to be parted from her – in life or in death. He knew she felt the same and wouldn't want to live without him. But then, a niggling doubt crept into the back of his mind. Would she?

His throat felt dry, and sweat stood on his forehead. Would everyone, including Violet, see this death pact as mere selfishness on his part? If he didn't take her with him, he knew Karen would always look after her mam - even when she invariably ended up in a care home. His beloved daughter would always give Violet the best, of that he was sure.

Lawrence caressed the top of Violet's hair, and she looked up at him, smiling with the docile expression on her face – ever trusting of him.

He thought of how the family was divided and knew Lucca and Karen would be devasted at his death, but perhaps not so much, Josh and Sam. And Violet? Well, once the dementia really took hold, she might not even remember who he was - or had been.

CHAPTER TWENTY ONE
The cottage near Chopwell Woods

I'm standing under the shower the next morning when I get shampoo in my eye and yelp. Climbing out, I struggle to open the top of the new tube of toothpaste and curse under my breath. Looking into the mirror above the hand basin, I take a few deep breaths and tell myself to calm down. I'm irritated with myself because I can't seem to solve this blooming case. Where the hell are they? I growl at the mirror before pulling a comb through my curls.

I think of the postcard which Josh showed us yesterday. His dad's words were stilted, and I reckon, as a last goodbye to his children, he could have said so much more. But is that just because he has a tetchy personality and belongs to what we would call the old-school brigade?

I remember my own father and how he was a man a of few words too. However, I do believe he would have thought of something more to say and would have mentioned my mother in his message, even though Lawrence had signed the card from them both. Since Lawrence appears to be a controlling man, perhaps Violet had no say in the matter.

Pulling a white dress over my head, I think of her letter tucked inside the library book. She had bared her soul to her children in true motherly fashion – much like my mother would have done for me. But I do wonder why she thought her end was close enough to address the envelope for after her death. And, as Karen had suggested, did something happen at Long Bank that forced them to leave. There must have been an underlying cause behind their disappearance. I grit my teeth while applying lipstick in the mirror.

Maybe it's time to step away from the case for a short while to clear my mind and reduce the stress and agitation that I'm feeling. I doubt I'll find anything at Chopwell, as the siblings have already been there, but I decide to enjoy the ride out and the countryside views in the meantime.

Muttering to myself, I say, 'I'll try one last time to look at their disappearance from a different angle, a fresh perspective that might lead to new insights at the cottage. If this doesn't bring anything more to light, I may have to concede defeat to Karen, charge her my fees, and leave the case to the police.'

I swallow hard with a sour taste in my mouth at the thought of doing this because I love getting to the crux of a matter. But this time, I may have to admit defeat. This will be the first case where I haven't found a solution – where I can't say what has happened, and where Violet and Lawrence have gone – but, I also know I'm not infallible.

Shortly after ten o'clock, with a long sigh, I climb into my car. This is the only place linked to the missing couple that I haven't yet visited, and set off to Chopwell with reliable, steady Doris giving me directions.

Chopwell Wood is about ten miles southwest of Gateshead, and the road entrance to the car park is in the Hookergate area of High Spen village, off the B6315. The entrance road narrows to single track around a blind bend, but I don't worry - Doris will keep me right.

As I follow her directions, my mind drifts back to last night. After another delicious meal of chicken kebabs in the hotel, I found Sam's page on Facebook. I browsed through her friends and photographs on different posts. It all looked like a typical young woman's social media - nothing surprising to note. Sam looked happy among her friends, most of whom seemed to be Goths too. Their photos were from the big Gothic weekend in Whitby, an annual event where they'd been having a great time.

I also checked UK missing persons statistics and was shocked to learn that someone is reported missing every ninety seconds. And there are over 170, 000 people reported missing every year. I shake my head in disbelief at these figures, and know that Karen, Josh, and Sam are far from being alone in their situation.

There were guidelines on a missing persons website which I read with interest. It tells families to acknowledge their feelings and stay busy by engaging in activities they enjoy to keep their minds occupied. I nod - Karen and Josh have definitely done this by running their business. Sam, not so much, but she has Karen's full support and help. They've stuck together, using their family bonds to cope with their own personal grief by being closer to each parent.

I suppose, in the months to come, even if Violet and Lawrence are not found, the siblings will go through the stages of grief as we all do - denial, anger, bargaining, depression, and, finally acceptance. It is still a seven year wait for a missing person to be presumed dead, unless in some situations, it may be possible to apply for a declaration of death earlier if there is substantial evidence that the person has died.

Waiting at traffic lights, I pull out my sunglasses as the sun is strong, and I'm squinting, which I know will give me a headache. I drive slowly down Derwent Street, a busy area lined with small shops. Apparently, Chopwell was traditionally a coal-mining area and was once known as, 'Little Moscow' due to strong support for the Communist Party. The council houses in the village are surrounded by beautiful countryside in a semi-rural setting.

I think of my small ground-floor flat in a terraced house, similar to these, and smile, longing for the peaceful atmosphere I've created at home.

When I first moved in, I told John, 'I'm not sure how long I'll be living here within the six-month rental, so I don't want to spend much money on the place.'

However, the landlord allowed me to paint the rooms in an ice-cream colour which is light yet soothing at the same time.

I'd never lived alone before, and at first, it felt strange and quiet with just me and Alfie during the day. But within a month I grew to love the flat. Just as Karen, Josh, and Sam think of this cottage as their safe haven, my flat has become mine.

The royalties I still receive from my books pay the rent, and the few sleuthing cases I've done have helped with my living expenses. And, of course when the Gosforth house is sold, I'll have a lump sum to keep as my safety blanket until I retire. Knowing this settles my mind. I dream of curling up on my squashy sofa with Alfie on a throw and a good book. Even though I'm not writing now, I still love reading books by my favourite authors.

I brought light voile drapes and cushions from the spare bedroom in Gosforth. Allan had been amenable but sour when he said, 'Just take what you want from our family home – it doesn't matter to me – it's just a house!'

However, I wanted a fresh start. I didn't want my new place to remind me of what I'd shared with him and our family. I wanted this place to be mine alone. The colour in the bedroom is highlighted with lemon bedding and accessories. John reckons the big cream candles in their holders create an intimate atmosphere, but I grin - that's probably wishful thinking on his behalf.

As I drive through Chopwell, hoping to fit more clues together, I decide to check with a local taxi company. If Lawrence and Violet aren't using their car, they must have got here somehow, that's if I can find any trace of them in the cottage. And John has suggested asking at a garage if anyone has seen their white Audi E3.

Following Doris's instructions, I turn down a lane and pull up outside Bluebell Cottage, which is well signposted. Climbing out of the car, I smile at the sight of the small, chocolate-box country cottage.

Leaving Alfie in the car, I whisper, 'Stay here for five minutes, and then we'll have a good run in the woods later.'

I know Karen, Josh, and Sam would have loved racing around here as kids, so Alfie and I will too. The area is densely populated with tall trees, and according to their website, there are 360 hectares of mixed woodland. The River Dee runs through, with little streams and wooden bridges to cross.

Suddenly, my heart begins to pound as I spot a white Audi parked at the side of the cottage, and know I've found the right place. I sigh, licking my dry lips. But are they still here, or is this going to be another dead end?

CHAPTER TWENTY TWO
Lawrence Braithwaite

Lawrence had woke that morning shortly after nine o'clock, knowing it would be the last day he would watch the sun come up. Sunrise had been early, being summertime, and he'd listened to birds in full chorus. Violet was tucked up away from him, sleeping on her side in the position they'd shared all their married lives.

Dressed in his blue short-sleeved shirt, knowing he'd need his arm free for the injection, he had decided these would be the clothes he would wear to die in.

At his final breakfast, he had fried smoked bacon and cracked a fresh egg into the frying pan, knowing the state of his coronary arteries no longer mattered. He had always loved the flavour combination of bacon and eggs - it had been one of their staple cottage breakfasts when the children were little. Although, Violet had always grilled the bacon and scrambled the eggs, mindful of their family's health.

She'd joined him at the smell of bacon frying, and they'd enjoyed breakfast together - him with yesterday's newspaper propped against the milk jug, and her book laid flat next to her tea cup, where she glanced over frequently to read a page. It was their daily ritual, with hardly a word spoken between them. He'd wondered if he should say something meaningful to her on this last occasion, but after all the years they'd been married, he figured it wasn't necessary. Violet had headed off to the bathroom to take a shower.

Alone again, he'd washed the dishes and then taken the insulin vial from the empty margarine tub in the fridge.

Next, he had retrieved the bottle of chloroform from the holdall and a small box with a syringe inside. He'd been ready to wait for her return - which she did, wearing a purple skirt and top that had always been one of his favourites. You'd think she knew, he had thought as he watched her sit down on the sofa and pick up her book.

Lawrence had sat down next to her. He had held the short note he'd written yesterday explaining his actions and then had tied a torniquet tightly around the top of his left arm. Closing his eyes, he had remembered every inch of the woman who sat beside him – the woman he had loved all his life.

CHAPTER TWENTY THREE
Finding Lawrence and Violet

I try the door handle and am amazed to see it open. I stop still in my tracks, thinking, this doesn't look good - unless of course, they're here, hiding out. However, I can't imagine Karen or Josh forgetting to lock up when they came two weeks ago. If not, could it be burglars? Local teenagers hanging around? I can almost hear John saying, "Wait for the police to come."

Opening my bag, I pull out a pair of disposable gloves and my notepad from the side pocket. As I put the gloves on, my warm and clammy hands make my thumb stick, and I tut in annoyance, eager to get inside.

Slowly, I push the door wider and creep inside. I need to call out but hesitate, conscious that they've never met me, and using their Christian names my be disrespectful. So instead, I shout, 'Mr Braithwaite! Mrs Braithwaite - are you here?'

No answer. There's utter silence. If they were here, surely there would be a TV or radio playing? A washing machine whirling? Or some sign of life. But there's isn't.

The door opens into a squat, open-plan room that appears empty. I take another two steps further inside, calling again, 'Helloooo!'

Facing me is the low back of a wood-framed sofa, with a TV in the corner. I don't need to go any further; I can see the tops of two grey heads above the checked material. There is no movement at all.

Gingerly, not knowing what I will find, I walk slowly around to the front of the sofa.

My heart lurches against my ribs, and sweat beads on my forehead as I see them sitting together, side by side, holding clasped hands.

A white cotton handkerchief with an embroidered L in the corner, and a note is on Violet's knee. Beside her leg is the missing framed photograph from the dressing table in their bedroom at Long Bank. Their heads are tilted back against the squashy sofa cushions as if simply watching TV.

I look at Lawrence with a syringe hanging out of a vein in his arm. I step closer. He's not breathing. In his short sleeved shirt, I feel for a pulse, but there's nothing. I can tell he is dead. I freeze, unsure what to do next. And then, the sound of a soft moan from Violet jolts me into action. Stepping around to her, I see she looks out of it but is still breathing, making faint whining noises.

I whip out my mobile and press Mira's number, praying, Oh, please answer, please answer quickly.

Taking a deep breath, my shoulders droop, and my fingers tremble as I hear her voice.

'Mira, it's Faye!' I shout. 'I've found them in the cottage!'

'What!'

I babble out what I've discovered, and she shouts back, 'Don't touch a thing - I'm on my way!'

'O...Okay.' I say, but I keep talking, my voice wobbling. 'G...Get an ambulance for Violet – she's still breathing!'

She ends the call, and I stand still, taking deep breaths. Looking from one to another, I note they look nothing like their happy, smiling faces in the photograph. Lawrence's face is white, sagging and bloated.

Sunlight streams through the side window, illuminating his protruding tongue with his eyes closed. He doesn't look peaceful at all. In fact, he looks tortured in some way with his forehead furrowed, and his thin lips twisted. I shiver remembering my dream.

Violet is pale with her eyes open, staring vacantly ahead into the room. I kneel beside her, taking her hand and squeezing it gently. 'You're okay, Violet. The ambulance is coming – stay with me.'

I'm not sure if this is the right thing to say, but I've seen it in TV dramas, and I reckon she's semi-conscious now.

I look around, knowing this could be a crime scene and don't move my feet anymore. I remember writing in my crime novels how crucial it is not to disturb anything - Mira has already warned me. Psychology in a crime scene flashes through my mind and I repeat it to myself: Use the same footsteps as the person in front, as if walking in deep snow. Keep to the edges of the room, away from the affray. Initially, no one should speak a word at a crime scene and should use the process of one in, one out.

Has there been an attack? There's no sign of a struggle - no upturned furniture, no scattered cushions. Nothing seems to be out of place. I sigh looking down at the note on Violet's purple skirt, itching to know what it says. Was this meant to be a double suicide pact? However, I know better than to touch the note.

I keep squeezing Violet's hand as she moans and start counting the minutes on my watch. I suppose, it could take fifteen to twenty minutes for help to arrive from

Gateshead. However, after just six or seven minutes, I hear a police car pull up, and a young PC rushes inside.

'Hello, I'm from our Chopwell neighbourhood police office. Help is on it's way,' he says. 'Just stay with the lady – you're doing great!'

Although I know he can't be, this lad looks about seventeen to me, his bright blonde hair making him seem even younger. His radio crackles as he hurries outside shouting back into it. Leaning to my left, I watch out of the window as he rolls out blue and white tape: POLICE DO NOT CROSS around the cottage, tying it to two large tree trunks.

And then I hear sirens outside. Here they come, I think, a lump forming in the back of my throat. It sounds like the cavalry are arriving. I breath out slowly and deeply, knowing I'm no longer alone, and that my tears aren't far away.

A middle-aged paramedic rushes inside, placing a reassuring hand on my shoulder. 'We've got this now, thanks. You've done well.'

His touch releases an unexpected wave of tension, making my mouth dry. I need to get out of their way, I think and sit back on my hunches. Gradually, I stand up feeling pins and needles tingle in my feet with being in a cramped position, and stamp them gently on the carpet.

A young female paramedic joins him, carrying two large bags of equipment. As they tend to Violet, I walk around the edge of the room to the doorway. Whilst they hook Violet up to monitors and place an oxygen mask on her face, they ask questions about her medical history. Of course, I don't know the answers but explain briefly how I found them, and that they've been missing for ten days.

The older paramedic lifts up the handkerchief, sniffs it, and tuts. 'Unless I'm mistaken, he has used chloroform to subdue her.'

I smile as the younger paramedic asks him what chloroform is, but I glance out of the window as more tyres crunch on the gravel. An unmarked police car screeches to a halt and an Asian woman climbs out. I reckon this has to be Mira Patel. Two more police cars pull up behind her.

She flies through the door and grabs my hand shaking it firmly. 'Hi, Faye, we've met at long last!'

I nod miserably. 'Yeah, I just wish it had been under better circumstances,' I say, and jerk my head to the side.

She hurries over to the paramedics and I watch her movements pacing around the sofa. Mira is pretty, with heavy, dark eyebrows, big brown eyes, and long black hair secured with a silver clasp. Her wide-legged brown trousers swish around flat shoes with blue covers on them as she paces. In a crisp shirt tucked inside these trousers, I figure she looks smart and professional. She rarely smiles, but when she does at the paramedic, who she obviously knows, I see big straight white teeth.

She asks him, 'So, what have we got here, then?'

The paramedic stands up and nods. 'I think Violet has had a handkerchief placed over her nose and mouth with chloroform on it to make her drowsy, but she's still alive and the oxygen is bringing her around. We'll blue-light her up to the QE hospital now,' he says, and then huffs. 'Her husband is obviously dead. There's an empty phial of old insulin which he's injected into his arm so this has done the job right enough.'

There's more kerfuffle at the front door as I watch a small white van pull up outside. A bald headed man climbs out of the front, while a younger guy opens the back and lifts out a grey metal case.

The young, blonde PC puts his head in the door and says, 'Boss, here's the crime scene manager.'

Dressed in white paper body suits, they stride under the tape and into the cottage. The bald headed man shouts, 'Everyone other than the paramedics get out of this room!'

Mira heads back to me, and I notice she's wearing blue disposable gloves while handling the letter in a clear plastic evidence bag. She jerks her head and I follow her stepping outside into the garden area. I notice the row of boots that Josh had mentioned and sigh – the siblings are all in for a horrible shock.

Mira reads aloud, 'Violet has been diagnosed with vascular dementia and we'd always made a pact that we could never live without each other. I couldn't bear to watch her suffer and be without her afterwards.'

I avert Mira's gaze and nod with a bitter taste in my mouth. I can't stop myself from thinking - how selfish is that? Or maybe, I cringe, Lawrence saw it as some kind of mercy killing? I shake my head and stare down at my sandals, knowing this poor woman had suffered at the hands of her deranged husband. Had she known what he was going to do? Is that why she addressed her pink envelope - to be read after my death?

I think of Lawrence now and try to find a smidgen of sympathy for him, but it's difficult. Although, in the end, when it came to the crunch, he obviously couldn't go through with killing her as well. So maybe, that's in his defence. I suppose, once a doctor, always a doctor.

I've been so lost in thought that I'm startled when Mira speaks.

'So,' she says, 'no matter what my inspector says when he gets here, from me, I'm eternally grateful for what you've done.'

She looks into my eyes and perhaps sees the disappointment I'm feeling, and the stony expression on my face. My insides feel like they have shrunk, and I have a hitching cough in my chest, as I say, 'Y…Yeah, but he's dead, and she is s…seriously ill!'

Mira places her hand on my shoulder and squeezes it. 'Look, you do realise that if Violet survives, you will have saved her life!'

I clench my jaw, and feel my stomach harden. 'I know,' I wail. 'But I spent this morning messing about in the shower, and if I'd come earlier - maybe at nine o'clock - then Lawrence might still be alive, too!'

The crime manager has stepped up behind us, heading out towards his van. He interrupts, saying, 'This man has been dead for at least seven hours, so I wouldn't beat yourself up about that.'

Mira shrugs. 'And they might not have been here yesterday – they could have arrived late last night, for all we know at this stage.'

The crime manager nods. 'Also, in my experience over the years, I know that if someone wants to kill themselves, they'll find a way, no matter what anyone does…'

I take a deep breath and pull back my shoulders. I thank them both and glance over to my car.

Remembering Alfie on the back seat, I decide a cuddle is in order and head towards him. Opening the passenger door, I slide in next to him and know he senses that I'm upset. He crawls into my lap like a baby and I slump into the seat burying my face into his soft fur. My eyes fill with tears and I murmur, 'Oh, Alfie, it was awful finding them like that.'

I'd been desperate to find Violet and Lawrence, and I had - but not in the way I, or anyone else for that matter, would have liked. I can't find much satisfaction in this outcome at all.

I watch as the paramedics rush Violet out of the cottage on a stretcher. Moments later, with blue lights flashing, the ambulance speeds off through the gap the police have created in the sealed-off area.

Glancing between the front seats and out through the windscreen, I look across to the woods and trees beyond. At the outskirts of the cottage grounds, a crowd of onlookers have gathered, mobiles held high in the air, hoping to snap photographs of the police vehicles and the crime scene manager's van.

I scowl and tug at the sleeve of my dress. What is it they want to see? I once read about accident or suicide tourists - people who linger at scenes of tragedy, eager to witness the aftermath of death or disaster. It's ghoulish. I certainly have no desire to see the remains of an old man's dead body or a seriously ill elderly woman. But clearly, these people do.

It also amazes me how quickly bad news spreads – faster than ever now, thanks to social media. The crowd is holding up their smart phones, trying to get closer shots, and I know there'll already be images of the woods circulating on Facebook and Twitter. What is it that fascinates people about tragedy and accidents? It's well known that drivers often cause further chaos by slowing down to gawk at road traffic accidents.

As this thought crosses my mind, I know social media must be flooded with speculation. It's time to ring Karen, Josh, and Sam. They need to here this from us, not see it on X or Facebook. I pause, trying to work out the kindest way to tell Karen that Lawrence is dead, and Violet is in a critical condition being rushed to hospital.

Feeling overwhelmed, I take a few deep breaths and set my jaw. John wouldn't want me to fall apart – he'd want me to get on with the job in hand. I reassure Alfie, then climb out of the car and head back inside the cottage doorway to voice my concern for the family to Mira.

But before I can speak, she takes over.

'I'm sending a PC to the siblings to inform them of what's happened. We never, if at all possible, deliver news of a relative's death over the phone. They need to make their way to the QE hospital to be with their mam.'

'Okay,' I say. 'I'll text Karen and tell her to find Sam, then go to Josh at the business premises to wait for the PC arriving.'

She nods in agreement.

Back in the car, I compose the message to Karen.
'Karen, there's been a development and I'm with Mira Patel. She wants you to find Josh and Sam and go to the business premises, where a PC will arrive shortly to update you on what's happened and what you need to do. I can't explain yet, but I'll be there later. Faye XX'

I think of Lawrence now and wonder what to do? Should I wait until they take his body away to the morgue at the QE hospital? Maybe Karen would like me to remain with him so he's not alone? I remember the first time we were in Long Bank house, how she'd filled with tears talking about him sitting in his armchair with the newspaper. Her usual composure had faltered, and in that moment, I could see how much she worshipped him. He was - or had been - her idol.

I decide she would want me to wait. Taking a swig from my bottle of water, I let Alfie on his lead out of the car while he does his business. Then I give him a drink before settling him back inside.

Sitting quietly, I go over everything that has happened in the cottage, my actions, and what comes next. I do hope Violet pulls through without lasting effects – though, in truth, I believe she has suffered an attack from her husband. Maybe Lawrence thought he was acting out of love, but his intentions were definitely warped.

After a while, I watch them bring out Lawrence on a trolley in a zipped black bag. I climb over to the driver's seat and turn the ignition, then drive away.

CHAPTER TWENTY FOUR
Grief personified

At four o'clock, I go back to the hotel felling exhausted and talk it all through with John on the phone. He wants to come over, but I refuse.

'No, I'll be okay,' I say.

'But you've had an awful shock, Faye!'

Probably for the first time today, I smile. His consideration for my feelings always astounds me because it's the first time in my life I've had someone totally on my side and looking out for me. Without taking control, his support and guidance are invaluable. In my past family life, I had to get over trauma and shocking events on my own, as Allan always leant on my shoulders to sort us out. Therefore, having John prop me up is wonderful.

'Yes, it was horrible, but I'm settling down now. I'm going to have a soak in the bath and a strong cup of coffee,' I say. 'I'll drive back to South Shields tomorrow morning.'

I'd told him how my next visit would be to see the siblings, who apparently are holed up in Karen's house now.

Josh had sent me a quick text to say, 'Mam is recovering well, and we are all looking forward to seeing you soon – please call down so we can thank you.'

'Okay,' John says. 'Just remember, you don't have to go and see them. The case is closed, and you could walk away without more upset,' he says. 'But I know you'll go, so I'll ring later and find out what happens when you've been to see them.'

I head into the bathroom and fill the tub with warm water and bubble bath. Sinking my shoulders into the water, Alfie wanders in, and I trail my hand over the edge of the bath to stroke his fur. 'So, Alfie,' I whisper, 'all my theories and suspicions about the three siblings were way off the mark. They had nothing to do with Violet and Lawrence's disappearance. I got it totally wrong.' I bite my lip. 'It was all down to the father of the family. I'd had no suspicions about him whatsoever, thinking he was just a rude, arrogant old doctor.'

Alfie whines, and I muse, how wrong could I have been? I thought I would feel elated if I found them, but this was not the ending I'd hoped for. It makes me doubt whether I'm any good at this sleuthing role and wonder if I should look for something else to throw myself into. I'm at that age where, Penny would say, 'the world is your oyster,' and I know that when I get home, I'll have to think hard about my future. As the water cools, I shake myself, climb out, and get dressed to head over to the restaurant.

After my last meal in the hotel, I climb into the car and drive once more to The Holly's, pulling up outside Karen's house. I remember the first time I arrived here, doubting myself and my ability to find the missing parents because it was something I hadn't undertaken before. Now, I still have mixed feelings about the outcome. Yes, I feel pleased that at least I hadn't given up - though I was close to doing so - but I persevered and eventually found them both. However, for one of them to be dead and the other to be ill in hospital, casts a cloud over the result.

Josh opens the door as I walk up the path and takes Alfie's lead from me. My dog seems to have a sixth sense for the aftermath we are about to face, which will certainly be a depressing atmosphere among them all. It's bound to be, I reckon, and know Karen will be the worst affected.

He leads me into the lounge and sits me down in one of the large armchairs while Alfie lies over my sandals. He doesn't approach Josh, Alice, or a tall young lad hovering in the corner of the room for petting - obviously staying close to watch over me.

Josh introduces Lucca, and I recognise him from his portrait on the wall of the sunroom. Although, of course, he doesn't look as smiley-faced, but who would when their grandfather had just died. From what I've heard about Lawrence, he would have been right up there on a pedestal in Lucca's eyes. But now, his grandfather had been knocked clean off the top.

In jeans and a T-shirt, he steps forward and shakes my hand politely. 'Uncle Josh rang me earlier, knowing something was wrong, and I begged a lift off a friend so I got home within the hour,' he says.

'It's good to meet you,' I say. 'I only wish it could have been under happier circumstances.'

He nods, and I see his big blue eyes full of sadness as he slopes back to the corner. 'Mam should have told me earlier what was going on,' he says. 'I'm not a ten year old!'

I smile. 'Aah, but that's our job as a Mam, Lucca. I would probably have done the same with my daughter.'

He shakes his head. 'I just can't believe he's died, and I didn't get the chance to say goodbye.'

'I know, it's been an awful shock for you all,' I say, looking around the room. 'It would have been bad enough if he'd died in normal circumstances, but this has been so hard.'

Lucca shuffles his feet. 'You're right. And to think Mam has been going though all of this on her own while I was with my friends down in York is even harder!'

Josh intervenes. 'Well, she's not been strictly on her own because we've stood by her, and of course, Faye has helped us all.'

In a pair of red shorts that look a few sizes too small for her, Alice says, 'I told Josh that Lucca needed to be here with his family, so he rang him.'

I wonder where Sam and Karen are and, more to the point, what state they're in when Josh answers my unspoken question.

Josh mutters, 'At the moment, Sam is at Mam's bedside in the hospital refusing to leave her. And our Karen is in there, trying to pull herself together,' he says, jerking his head over his shoulder.

I reckon he means the sunroom, and I nod. 'It's certainly been a horrible time for you all, and it'll take a while to come to terms with what's happened.'

Josh sits forward and puts his head in his hands, saying, 'This has been a living hell!'

I hope he isn't going to cry, and I try to think of something positive to say. 'So, how is Violet doing? The last time I saw her, she was being driven off in the ambulance.'

Alice moves to Josh's side and strokes the back of his hair. She says, 'Well, Violet is conscious, and we are all thrilled that the paramedics could revive her.

And, of course, they told us what you'd done by keeping her going until they got there.'

My cheeks flush, and I swallow hard. 'Em, I didn't do anything but squeeze her hand and keep talking to her, Alice,' I say. 'So please don't think that - I did nothing towards her medical condition.'

Alice says, 'But she would have known you were there and she wasn't alone, which means a lot.'

I want to tell them Violet was too far out of it to know whether I was there or not, but I don't want to drag them down again, so I say nothing.

Josh looks up, his face changing, and cries jubilantly, 'Oh, Faye, you saved our mam's life!'

I shake my head, but he gets up and begins to pace the room. 'If you hadn't gone to the cottage to double check, they'd still not be found. And, the doctors said it was a close call, so without you, she would be dead too!'

Alice turns to me. 'We are all very grateful, Faye. And when Violet is physically better, I've arranged for a week of respite in Lindisfarne care home, which will give her time to take stock of what happened. She won't want to be alone in their Long Bank house at the moment. The hospital doctors have explained that the effects of chloroform on the liver and kidney can last up to forty-eight hours, so they are keeping a close eye on her. They've also explained about vascular dementia - how she's been through a traumatic experience, which is bound to confuse and upset her,' she says, and then sighs. 'And, of course, she'll have to decide what to do about Lawrence's funeral, which we think might be in his will.'

I figure Alice is taking on these arrangements at the moment, as, strictly speaking, she's not direct family. She is the calm, controlled person amongst them. I smile at her and nod.

'It's good to have a plan in mind, Alice, and I know later everyone will be grateful for your forethought.'

Out of the corner of my eye, I watch Lucca slope into the sunroom and then reappear a few minutes later.

'Faye,' he says. 'My mam would like to see you.'

He holds open the door to the sunroom, and I enter quietly. Karen is sitting on the sofa, looking out into the garden, and the only word I can use to describe the look on her face is ravaged.

In crumpled linen trousers and a black T-shirt, she is dishevelled, to say the least. Her usual meticulous hair is standing on end as she runs her fingers through it, and streaks of mascara stain her cheeks.

I feel an ache in my throat as my heart goes out to her. I'm not even sure Karen knows it's me, but I perch on the chair opposite. She must feel Alfie put his paw onto her knee, as he's done before, because she bends down to him and buries her face in his fur.

Lifting her head again, she looks across to me and nods. 'Hello, Faye,' she croaks.

Her voice sounds ragged, probably with crying, I think, and I smile at her.

'I'm so very sorry, Karen,' I offer.

Karen's world and her love for her father is shattered, which is understandable.

I ask, 'Would you like to know exactly what happened?'

I know from psychology research I've done in the past that people like to know the exact facts in a traumatic event, so slowly and carefully, I explain what happened in the cottage and my actions.

'So, the police are convinced that no one else was involved in what happened.'

She lets Alfie go and jumps up from the sofa. Karen's nostrils flare, and she sweeps an arm wide. 'No!' she shouts. 'It was all down to Dad!'

She shakes her head wildly. 'I just can't believe he was capable of doing this!'

I recognise the denial and anger of grief and loss. She is furious and stamps her foot like a child. 'I mean, trusting your doctor is set in stone – it goes without saying that they'll always do the right thing for you,' she rages. 'So, how could he want to do that to Mam, especially when he knew she had the beginnings of dementia?'

I shake my head as Alfie creeps back to my side, and I stroke his ears in comfort.

'What happened at the cottage is a hell of a shock for you all, Karen,' I say, knowing my words sound feeble. 'But at least your dad, the doctor, couldn't do what he'd planned and, in the end, saved your mam.'

'Hmmph! The Dad I knew and loved would never have even thought about doing that to her, or anyone else for that matter. He would have fought tooth and nail to save anyone's life because, as a doctor that's what he was trained to do – so, why?' she shouts and begins to pace around the furniture. 'In God's name – why!!'

I recall the image of him in the chair and slowly shake my head. 'Maybe he, too, was suffering from some sort of breakdown?' I say, trying to catch her hand as she passes, but I miss her. 'However, one thing is for sure: he loved her enough not to witness her decline and couldn't bear to live without her.'

Karen murmurs, 'Mam said only last year that he'd been different since he retired, but I thought she'd meant in a good way – that he was happy to have left work.'

I shrug. 'Well, retirement is a massive life change to deal with, and maybe he suffered from poor mental health but, being the head of the family, he didn't want to admit this to anyone, especially his children.'

I hope this may help in some way but doubt it at the moment. When she's calmed down and can think more clearly, other people's words may sink in and help to re-order her thought processes.

She turns and slumps back down into the chair. Leaning forward, I can see she has run out of steam. She whispers, 'What did he look like, Faye?'

I take a deep breath and sigh. Thinking of his bloated face and twisted mouth, I need to soften the blow and decide to tell her a version of the truth. 'He was peaceful, Karen,' I say. 'He looked at peace in the cottage.'

She nods and then almost growls, 'Well, grandfather or not, we are putting up that bloody cottage for sale. None of us, including Mam, will ever want to set foot in the place ever again! Alice has arranged for a removal firm to go and empty all the belongings, both from olden days and the few recent things Mam and Dad had taken up there.'

We both turn and see Lucca in the doorway. 'Mam, if I make some toast and fresh tea, will you please eat and drink something?'

I stand up to leave and glance at the mug on the table, full of undrunk tea. 'Yes, Karen, you should at least drink fluids,' I say. 'And for once, let Lucca look after you for a change.'

Karen sits up and takes my hand at the doorway. 'Thanks, Faye,' she says. 'We'll be in touch.'

Josh sees me out of the front door as I clip Alfie into his harness. He looks tormented and mutters, 'Dad was a tyrant when we were growing up. He was respected in Birtley because he was a good doctor and looked intellectual, but at home, he was grumpy and curt when we were young. I once heard Mam shout at him, "It was her family who'd owned and ran the funeral business, which had supplied the money to buy the house! And how Mam had kept it going, knowing any of their three kids would always have employment!"'

I know Josh is hard to gauge because his face changes quickly from one expression to another. He could be congratulating himself that he'd been right all along - that his dad hadn't been a good man - although I think that's debatable and none of the past difficulties between them had been his fault.

Of course, Sam and Josh have had troubled relationships with their dad, and I know they won't be as crestfallen as Karen is, but maybe, going forward it'll give them their own set of daemons to deal with.
They've now lost the chance to find out why Lawrence wasn't close to them and if there'd been a way to put this right.

I sigh. My role here is finished, and I could walk away, but feel the need to help in whatever way I can. 'Look, Josh,' I say. 'This has got to be so difficult for you all to cope with.'

He shakes his head. 'I can't believe he took the easy way out and thought only of himself rather than caring for Mam!' A single big tear rolls down his cheek. 'I think I'll spend the rest of my life hating him for what he was going to do to her.'

I pat his arm. 'But he didn't, Josh,' I say. 'So try to remember that when it came to the crunch, he couldn't do it!'

CHAPTER TWENTY FIVE
Going home to South Shields

At ten the next morning, dressed in my jeans and white shirt, I stand in the hotel reception, paying for my room, my car packed up ready for the drive back home to South Shields. I hadn't slept well last night, haunted by the image of Lawrence and Violet's faces staring into oblivion on the sofa. However, after a hot chocolate, I'd managed to soothe myself with the thought of being curled up next to John tonight.

Doris is giving me her instructions, and I smile, delighted that I'm homeward bound, driving back over the Tyne Bridge. So much happened in the past week - it's enough to make my head swim - but I focus on the road and traffic ahead. It's raining today, and the windscreen wipers are rhythmically swiping away the droplets from the windscreen.

Reaching the coast, I drive along South Shields seafront just as the sun breaks through the clouds. Turning onto the street to my flat, I whisper to Alfie, 'Home again, at last!'

I know he'll be desperate for a run in North Marine Park once I've unpacked. But know we'll have a few hours to ourselves while John is finishing up at work.

I remember the first day I moved in here, arriving with suitcases, bags, and a few small pieces of furniture. John had been standing outside the door, and the moment I climbed out of my car, I had unashamedly ran to him. He'd picked me up, swing me around in the air, whooping loudly – completely out of character for him, which told me how excited he was.

I turn the key in my door just as my neighbour appears, carrying a huge bouquet of flowers towards me. He tells me they were delivered at eight o'clock this morning, and I thank him for accepting them.

Inside the lounge, I lay the bouquet on the table and read the card. They're from Karen, Josh, and Sam, with a beautiful thank-you card in which they've each written separately, expressing their gratitude for saving their mam's life. I know Alice will have chosen and arranged the flowers. After hauling my holdall inside, I fill three vases with them, inhaling their gorgeous scent from each one.

With a cup of tea in hand, I ring Penny to let her know I'm home and to tell her what happened in the cottage.

She calls out, 'WOW! Faye, you saved that woman's life – you're our local heroine!'

I smile at her dramatic reaction. 'Yeah, it's just a shame their father was already dead but the coroner said he'd been gone for about eight hours, so I was too late.'

Penny cries, 'But if you hadn't gone, they could have been there forever and not found at all!' she says. 'It's time for a clap on the back, methinks.'

I laugh at her wit. 'And I've just had a call from my niece, Zoe - who is friends with Sam from university. Apparently, Sam is raving about me and how amazing I was in Birtley, especially for finding her mam alive.'

'Well, that's a glowing recommendation for further cases, Faye!'

Penny had worked in HR for years, and I smile, recognising her professional mindset kicking in.

I agree, deciding to stop resisting everyone's praise – it's something I've never been good at.

I can hear my mother's voice saying, 'You should blow your own trumpet more often.' And, I know she's right. I have a done a good job, though I can't shake off the regret that I wasn't able to stop Lawrence from taking his own life. But I console myself with the coroner's words; if someone is determined to end their life, they will.

Penny says, 'Well, I'm not surprised at your success - you have more intelligence and spirit than any of us!'

I feel my cheeks flush, thank her, and then end the call, promising to ring at the weekend.

John arrives later in the afternoon, and I throw myself into his arms. After a takeaway pizza and glasses of wine, we curl up on the sofa together. He twirls a tendril of my hair between his fingers and asks, 'Has this case been depressing? You've sounded a bit flat on the phone - not your usual cheery self.'

'Not really,' I say. 'It's been more frustrating than anything. I couldn't solve the mystery and was on the verge of giving up - and you know that's not me.'

'Yeah, just like last year in the guest house – you wouldn't give up, even when I was sick of getting nowhere with tracing the killer.'

Alfie creeps up to us, puts his paw on my knee, and pats it while John laughs.

'Even he looks proud of you – as if he is saying, well done.'

Of course, John has told me many times over the phone how impressed he is.

I lift my chin and smile. 'Well, I do feel proud of myself. I solved the case mostly through sheer good luck and perseverance,' I say. 'At first, I felt bad that I hadn't got there earlier, but the paramedic confirmed that, no matter what time I arrived, Lawrence would have been dead within ten minutes of the insulin injection.'

John says, 'It's a good job you had one last shot at it – otherwise, they would have been left there forever, and Violet would have died too. You saved her life, Faye, and that's something special.'

'The paramedic also said, if I hadn't turned up that day, Violet would almost certainly have died. He thought we'd just caught her in time.'

John sighs. 'Faye, in this line of detective work, unfortunately, there aren't many happy endings.'

I smile, knowing he's trying to make me feel better. 'Yes, but even in the crime books I wrote, I always strived for, if not a happy ending, then at least a satisfactory one – it's what readers prefer.'

He shrugs. 'Maybe for Lawrence, who didn't want to live any longer – this was satisfactory.'

I know this is the flip side of the coin that John always tries to instil in me, and I have to agree. It's not satisfactory for those left behind, but for Lawrence, it was.

I sigh, remembering that night in Birtley at the Alioli restaurant, discussing Pure Cremation. And I know we need to talk about death. Once again, I sense we are on the same wavelength - the subject feels like a silent elephant in the room between us.

John asks, 'So, has it been miserable, working with death and funerals all the time over there?'

I shrug. 'Not really. The family just accept death as part of life – which I suppose it is. And of course, it's their business; they have to make money and keep it afloat,' I pause. 'But in a way, I'm glad I've done it. It's made me think of my own demise - and yours.'

'Yeah, it's something we need to talk about, isn't it? I knew I'd upset you in the restaurant without meaning to, but as you just said, death is part of our lives. In some respects, it's something the police face every day at work. It could happen at any time – even more so these days.'

I swivel around and look up to his face. 'Yes, it'll be good to talk it through.'

John sighs. 'Well,' he says. 'Over the years, I've been slapped and spat at as a young PC, and I once twisted my ankle chasing a villain down a back lane. But thankfully, nothing serious. That said, society is more violent and aggressive now - where knives and guns are everywhere. I'm always reminding my team to be careful, and try to safeguard them as much as possible.'

I smile at his considerate nature, even though I know he's often gruff and shouts at them. His team, however, know he thinks highly of them and always has their backs.

All the same, the words knife and gun make me shudder again. The thought of him being seriously injured churns my stomach, but as Penny often says, 'It's time to pull on your big girl's pants and deal with it!'

I nod and say, 'Well, I've been thinking about this, and the TV advert which says Pure Cremation is "my funeral, my way" and that the ashes are returned to the family. So, I think, if and when my turn comes, this sounds the best option for Olivia and the girls to deal with.'

He cuddles me close and kisses the top of my head. 'Well, it's something that, whenever it happens for both of us, we'll sort it out together.'

As we head into the bedroom, I say, 'I'm going to ring Allan tomorrow to say I'm adding this to my will and see if he will do the same with his for Olivia.'

The next day, I ring Allan, and we talk about the final divorce, and agree to add to our wills that whatever is left after either or both of us die will all go to Olivia and the grandchildren. I visit the solicitor, who adds my wishes to my will. Instead of feeling sad, I feel content, knowing I now have things in place. If nothing else, my case in Birtley has made me get my ducks in a row, as they say. I also make Penny the executer in my will and ask her to look after Olivia, who has always called her aunty Penny.

***

The following week, I'm sitting on the beach while John has Alfie, wearing his life jacket, on the back of his paddleboard in the sea. Alfie is loving the water, and we discovered after the first time that he is a better swimmer than I am. Of course, I also know he is as safe as houses with John. Alfie would never have gone on a paddleboard with Allan.

I look out to sea and let my thoughts wander. Sam is the only sibling I hadn't seen since the day at the cottage. Out of everything I learned in Birtley, I'm sure there was some secret surrounding her or a mysterious happening in her past.

Just as I'm thinking this, a text arrives from Karen.

'My father's funeral is next Friday, and I'm praying you'll be free to come back for the service. You are to be our guest of honour because, without you, we would never have found our parents.'

I sigh at first and think, is this something I really want to do? But know I must. and reply, 'Yes, of course, I'll come back for the funeral to see you all.'

195

CHAPTER TWENTY SIX
The Braithwaite funeral

I'm in the car with John, driving over to Birtley for the last time. He has the afternoon off work and has insisted on coming with me to the funeral. I steal a look at him from the corner of my eye, wondering if he thinks I'll be tempted to stay here again and not return to South Shields. Which, of course, I wouldn't.

Penny had been right when she'd said absence makes the heart grow fonder, and I know he really missed while I was away for the week. As I had him - and I'd shown him how much on numerous occasions.

I grin, appreciating his black suit, white shirt, and black tie. He certainly looks respectful and smart for the occasion. I hope I do too, in my plain black dress and flat black pumps. I have a feeling this is going to be a funeral to remember, and the whole town of Birtley may well turn out in response.

John glances at me when we stop at traffic lights and rubs his chin. 'I've often wondered what drives people to take their own lives? I mean, he must have been pretty desperate to do it?'

I shrug. 'I suppose no one knows what goes through someone's mind in a mental heath crises. It wasn't a spur-of-the-moment decision, though, because he obviously planned it – he left a note and made preparations. Of course, being a doctor, he would know the best way to do it, choosing insulin as the drug to use,' I say. 'And he did send the postcard to say goodbye to the children in his own way.'

John nods. 'Yeah, and you often find the younger generation choose different ways out - driving too fast and crashing, or throwing themselves in front of high-speed trains.'

He shuffles in his seat, clearly feeling the heat in the dress trousers as the sun beats down on the windscreen. 'I know, but he was a doctor, so you'd think he would appreciate life more?'

'Well, he might have been a doctor, but he was still just a man, with all the same flaws as the rest of us.'

We pull up to the crematorium gates and drive slowly along to the car park at the back, out of respect. I remember coming here with Karen on my first day in Birtley. I'd been impressed with her self-control and restraint, despite the turmoil of her parents being missing.

But the last time I saw her, after returning from the cottage, she was a gibbering wreck. She had idolised her dad. I wonder how she has coped with his fall from grace - and how she'll get through today. Will she finally let go and break down in floods of tears, or will she manage to keep her stiff upper lip?

Within minutes, around thirty to forty people have gathered along the path in the centre of the crematorium gardens. Then we all turn and look to the gates as the funeral procession arrives.

John is chatting to an old man behind him, who tells us they've brought Mr Braithwaite from the house on Long Bank, stopping all the traffic on Durham Road. I wonder if Violet is well enough to attend the funeral with the rest of the family in the cars.

I gasp in shock, and have to admit, admiration at the sight before me. Karen and Josh are funeral conductors, walking very slowly in front of Lawrence's coffin along the path towards the crematorium doors. They both stand still, face each other, then turn to the coffin bowing deeply.

Josh is wearing a black three-piece suit and a black felt top hat, his face is pale. Karen looks equally - if not more – impressive. She's wearing a black skirt which I know is usually worn for a cremation, whereas female conductors wear trousers for burials. Her outfit is completed in a dark grey herringbone fitted jacket with black velvet lapels and large black buttons. A black bowler hat with matching velvet trim and a short black lace veil on the back is stylish and fits the occasion perfectly. I reckon she looks quite regal. Her back is ramrod straight, and I can see she is holding herself together in true family honour.

I whisper to John, 'The conductor title goes back to mediaeval times and is a mark of respect for the deceased. It's a bit like *A Christmas Carol* – the old Scrooge film and how Marley was buried.'

He grins, and nods at me then takes my hand in his.

Sam and Ellie look almost gothic, with Lucca between them in a dark grey suit, leading the funeral procession behind the hearse. Another fifty or so people follow - obviously locals from Birtley, many of the men wearing black armbands on their left arms. I wonder how many of them were his old patients. The town will have been agog with news of the tragedy. It's an old family business, after all, and their reputation speaks for itself.

There are no more cars behind the hearse, and I still can't see Violet anywhere.

Four pallbearers lift the coffin from the hearse and carry it inside. Their expressions and careful movements make it clear they feel honoured to do this.

The old man behind John whispers, 'Two of the pallbearers used to work for the business years ago, and have a high regard for the family. The other two were old friends of Lawrence.'

John nods in response as the old man removes his flat cap and bows his head.

'Aye,' the man says, 'we lost a good doctor in Birtley when he retired. He saved my wife's life years ago when many would have given up on her. But Doctor Braithwaite didn't. And I'll always be grateful for that.'

The pallbearers bring Lawrence inside, and we all follow. The room is long, with ten dark wooden pews are on either side of the central aisle, covered in blue carpet. John and I squeeze onto the end of a pew in the middle, and I look around.

Three arched windows are on either side allow enough sunlight to filter in, though hanging chandeliers provide additional lighting. The aisle leads down to a small platform, where a large brown wooden catafalque holds the coffin. I know the heavy, dark brown brocade curtains will slowly and automatically close at the end of the service.

Karen, Josh, Sam, Ellie, and Lucca sit in the front pew on the right. I notice that there's still no sign of Violet. Maybe she wasn't well enough to attend?

The coffin is made of plain wood, with panelled sides and brass handles. A single long cross of white flowers rests on top – Alice, no doubt, would have designed it with the local florist.

John leans in and whispers, 'That's a lovely piece of walnut – no expense spared there.'

I nod. 'Yeah, they've certainly pulled out all the stops.'

During the service, I know that I've done the right thing by not choosing this celebration-of-life cremation. I wouldn't want Oliva to go through this. If my demise was to happen soon, my two granddaughters would be scared at the closure of the automatic curtains. I smile to myself, thinking of them at such an impressionable age.

Shaking myself back to the here and now, I realise this was probably exactly what Lawrence wanted. Most older people do prefer a traditional service. Two classical pieces of music play from a loop, a short recap of his life is given, and Josh reads a piece of poetry.

Karen stands up, bows her head to the coffin once more, and speaks at the lectern. In a quiet but dignified voice, she says, 'We'd like to thank everyone for coming to pay their respects, the police for this investigations, and a special thanks to Faye Chambers, who has helped the whole family through this difficult time.'

I glance around, recognising a few familiar faces I met during my time in Birtley - the man from the library, the two women from Morrison's café, with Mary sitting at the front next to the Braithwaite's neighbour, Daisy, and Violet's friend from the bowling green.

They all nod and smile at me as John squeezes my hand tighter. Although I've tried to accept praise from everyone since the tragedy in the cottage, my cheeks burn. I shuffle on the hard wooden pew, feeling my dress stick to my legs. I attempt a smile in return, but sweat forms on my top lip, and I swallow hard.

And then, the curtains begin to close.

The family all rise first, leaving the front pew. Josh's face has changed to one of relief, while Sam wipes away a few tears as Ellie comforts her. Karen is still ramrod straight. She places a steading hand on Lucca's shoulder. He looks visibly upset but follows her lead, pulling back his young, slim shoulders and lifting his chin.

Pew by pew, everyone slowly leaves the room, and I'm relieved to be back outside in the sunshine.

The family stand in a row at the doorway, shaking hands and quietly accepting their condolences.

When it is our turn, I'm surprised when Karen wraps her arms around me into a big hug. 'I hope you didn't mind me saying that in there, but honestly, we couldn't have got through any of this without you!'

'No, I didn't mind - it's all okay, Karen. And it was a lovely service. You've done him proud with the procession.'

I realise that she hasn't met John, and I introduce them.

She takes John's hand and shakes it firmly. 'I hope you know what a lucky man you are to have Faye,' she says, smiling.

John returns the handshake and nods. 'Oh, believe me, Karen, I do.'

'I can't believe how many people have come,' she says, looking around the gardens.

I follow her gaze. 'Well, obviously, your dad was very well thought of in Birtley.'

A shadow crosses her face. 'Yeah, right - if only they knew what he'd done.'

I take her hand and squeeze it tight. 'Look, Karen, try to remember his good works as a doctor in the community and the dad you loved all your life before any of this happened.'

She nods. 'Yes, you're right. Dad has found his resting place, and Mam will join him when she's ready.'

I can tell she's starting to come to terms with her loss – or as much as one can ever do in such tragic circumstances when she's lost her dad. Wanting to shift the focus, I ask after Violet's health.

Karen smiles. 'Mam is in Lindisfarne care home and settled now – she's much better, thanks to you.'

Suddenly, from behind, I feel arms wrap around my waist. And, in a rare show of affection, Sam hugs me and cries, 'Oh, Faye, thank you so much for helping my mam – you brought her back to us!''

Realising it's the first time I've seen since the day in the cottage, I gently unwrap myself from her arms. 'It's okay, Sam, and I'm so pleased your mam is on the mend now.'

Sam turns back to Ellie, who takes her arm and leads her away.

I hope that now the siblings know exactly what happened, it has settled their minds and brought them some peace. Karen, at least, no longer seems tortured by the unknown.

As I glance down the path, I notice a tall, thin man standing on his own. He doesn't seem to know anyone here in Birtley.

Karen follows my eyeline and whispers, 'I haven't a clue who he is. At first, I thought he might be an old cousin or uncle, but if so, surely I'd know him – and I don't.'

The man turns around to face us, but his gaze is fixed firmly on Sam, now standing just behind Karen. I look at the features on his face and then rest my eyes back onto Sam. Their faces are identical, and I gasp in shock. And here's another secret in the family, I think.

I wonder if the others, especially Sam, have noticed the resemblance. They don't seem to have, and before I can say anything, Josh steps up to us. He shakes my hand, as does Alice, while I thank them for the flowers - and for paying my invoice promptly.

Alice says, 'We are having a wake in Birtley Community Centre if you'd like to join us?'

John looks down at his shoes, and I know he's not keen. Neither am I, for that matter. I politely decline, offering a small white lie that John has to get back to work.

Karen turns around to me, and says, 'Although mam didn't want to come to the funeral, she would like to meet you. I was wondering if you'd be able to visit her – it might help?'

I turn to John raising my eyebrow, knowing I can't refuse this request.

He smiles. 'Yes, that's fine - there's plenty of time.'

CHAPTER TWENTY SEVEN
Violet in Lindisfarne care home

John drives us back onto Durham Road, and we pull into the Lindisfarne car park. 'I won't be long – ten minutes, tops,' I say.

Pressing the buzzer on the inside door and speaking into the intercom, I let them know I'm here to see Violet Braithwaite. A care worker comes to greet me and takes me along the corridor and outside to a small balcony over looking the back of the fire station and park. I recognise Violet, who looks one hundred percent better than the last time I saw her in the cottage, and more like the original photograph I'd carried around with me while searching for them.

'And, you must be, Faye,' she says, patting the wooden garden chair next to her.

I smile and slide onto the chair. 'Yep, that's me.'

In a pale blue flowery dress, she smiles. 'Now, my children tell me that I've got you to thank for saving my life,' she says, dipping the rim of her sunhat against the glare.

The sun is hot on the balcony, and I wish I had my sunglasses. 'Well, it was the paramedics who saved you. All I did was hold your hand and talk to you because I didn't know what else to do.'

'You know, Faye, I've no memory of that at all – my only memory is of waking up in the hospital.' She says. 'But I thank you from the bottom of my heart.'

'That's okay, Mrs Braithwaite. I was glad to help in anyway possible.'

She nods. 'Yes, and call me, Violet,' she says. 'Our Karen told me you'd been all over Birtley looking for us, and I can only thank God for you coming here and getting involved.'

I grin. 'Well, you weren't easy to find, but I got my first lead at Saltwell Park and Beamish, so we knew you were around somewhere.'

She shakes her head. 'You'll think I'm awful for not coming to my husband's funeral, but when the police showed me his note and how he'd intended to take me with him, well I simply couldn't!'

I lean over to her hand on the chair arm and pat it. 'Don't upset yourself,' I say. 'It's a lot to come to terms with, and I think you're better off here, where it's quiet and you can focus on getting better first.'

Tears well in her eyes. 'I knew he was up to something because you don't live with someone for years without knowing when they're behaving strangely, but this?'

I think of Allan and how he hid from me the fact from me that he hadn't been divorced when we married, and I understand the shock she is feeling. I nod but struggle to think of what to say. I mutter, 'It's more than understandable after what you've been through, Violet.'

I feel her hand trembling under mine and squeeze it firmly.

She takes a deep breath. 'Our Karen has explained the particular type of dementia I've got, which, in a way, is a relief because I know my memory has been getting worse. Some days, like today, I can remember everything and know I'm lucid, but some days are worse, and I struggle to think properly, and sort out what clothes to wear and what needs washing.'

I know the difference between vascular dementia and Alzheimer's is often diagnosed with a brain scan because it's happened to Penny's aunt. Unlike Alzheimer's disease, the most significant symptoms of vascular dementia tend to involve speed of thinking and problem-solving rather than memory loss.

Hoping to console her, I nod. 'I think it's normal to have short-term memory loss, Violet, but can you remember everything from when you were younger?'

'You've got it in one,' she says and gets up slowly from her chair. With her arm outstretched wide over the balcony railing, she continues, 'I can see our funeral business from here – it's where I started work at fifteen with my mother. I can remember the clothes I wore that day and how she'd said, "Don't be frightened of the dead bodies because they won't do you any harm in life; it's the buggers walking about that can hurt you!"'

I laugh at the old saying and step around two big plant pots to stand next to her. I lay my hand on her shoulder. 'Oh yes, I thought I recognised the park, but we are standing behind it now, and I'd lost my direction for a moment.'

We talk about the business premises and the cemetery. 'I enjoyed meeting Josh, Alice, Karen, and Sam. They do a great job of running the place, and Sam is an amazing artist from what I've heard, but she does have her problems, doesn't she?'

Violet looks at me from the corner of her eye. 'I can tell you're a smart woman, Faye,' she says and then turns to face me. 'You know that Sam is different, don't you?'

My mouth dries, and I feel my stomach flip. What does she mean? That she appears to be a little autistic?

I'm not sure but remember the man at the funeral and, at the risk of upsetting her further, decide to speak my mind.

It might help her to talk to someone about Sam. 'Well, I saw a man at the funeral who looked more like Sam than any of your family ever could?'

She nods. 'I thought you'd guessed something,' she says. 'His name is Malcolm Jenkins, and you're right - he is Sam's Dad.'

I raise an eyebrow. 'And she doesn't know?'

Violet shakes her head. 'She doesn't, Faye. I thought he might turn up because Sam had put a post on Facebook saying her dad was dead and her mam was in a nursing home. Then yesterday, a sympathy card arrived from Malcolm. Karen asked who it was from, and I told them it was just from an old schoolfriend who moved to Cambridge and must have seen Facebook. It would have been easy for him to find out where and when the funeral was.'

'I see. And you still don't think she should know?'

Violet sighs heavily. 'Oh, Faye, I'm tired of lying and keeping it a secret,' she says. 'I've worried since she was born that I'd be found out and judged by everyone, but maybe now that Laurie has gone, it's time to come clean and just tell them all.'

A lightbulb moment pings in my mind, and I tilt my head while raising an eyebrow. 'Do you think your husband knew about Sam—that she wasn't his?' I ask. 'It might have influenced his initial plan to take you with him in the cottage.'

Violet shakes her head, chewing the inside of her cheek. 'No,' she says. 'There was only one letter a couple of months ago, and I burned it within minutes of it arriving while he was at the pool swimming, so I know he didn't see it!'

My muscles tense, and I can't help thinking this might have played a part in his tragic circumstances and demise in the cottage. Although, I shrug my shoulders—what does it matter now?

A lump forms in my throat as I look at this old woman and all she is going through. It's such a pity that, in the past, women felt forced to keep births a secret and that babies born out of wedlock were seen as shameful. We've come a long way since then, I think, and decide to make a suggestion. 'Maybe it would be a good idea to introduce Sam to Malcolm? With Lawrence gone, and when you eventually join him in the cemetery, she'll have someone else to rely on—another built-in family to help with her special needs.'

Violet stares ahead over the park. 'You're right. I do know that Malcolm has another daughter called Anne.'

I brighten. 'Well, that'll be another sister for Sam, won't it?'

She smiles and pulls back her slight shoulders. 'Yes. I'll tell them all the truth—the time for secrets is well and truly over!'

Violet walks towards the balcony doorway. 'I'm tired now, so I'll go back to my room,' she says. 'And once again, thank you for coming, Faye.'

I follow her out and leave through the main doors, spotting John sitting in his car, waiting patiently. I breathe in the fresh summer air.

He climbs out of the car, and I hug him tightly. Taking my hand, he squeezes it firmly and says, 'Come on, let's get you home.'

I know he was concerned last night when I'd been upset. He had warned me about getting too close to the people I work for—and he'd been right.

'Yes, let's go home. My time here in Birtley is over.'

Printed in Great Britain
by Amazon